The Dancer - A Murder Mystery

The Williams Family Cases, Volume 1

RoseMary Covington Morgan

Published by RoseMary Covington Morgan, 2024.

Table of Contents

To my friends and family. Thanks for your continuous support and patience while reading my many drafts of this story.

To "My Crew": Gina, Michael, Megan, Kevin, Jada, Ray and Kayla. I love you more than you can know.

The Dancer

RoseMary Covington Morgan

I was a chair dancer. No, not the sit on your lap and wiggle kind of chair dancer. I was the woman you see at a party, never on the dance floor, seated against a wall or at a table, dancing because she just couldn't help it. Yep, that was me, alone in a chair, shaking my shoulders, tapping my toes, and discreetly bouncing my butt to the beat of whatever rhythmic selection was playing.

Sometimes, a sympathetic soul would see me chair dancing, offer a hand, and guide me to the dance floor. I am not very good on the dance floor. I might try to shuffle my feet for a short time, but I couldn't wait to get back to my chair and dance where I'm most comfortable—sitting on my butt.

Slow songs were hard for me. Swaying back and forth in my chair to romantic lyrics lamenting lost love or recounting new love is uncomfortable and looks awkward. But there I was, sitting alone, swaying to the moans and whines of some popular singer when my future husband asked me to dance.

I accepted his offer. He was a good dancer and didn't seem to mind that I liked to lead.

That's the first thing I liked about him. Many men got frustrated as we stumbled on each other's feet. They would, with little hesitation, lead me back to my chair. But not my Anthony. We danced to three slow songs, then let loose on a few fast ones. I was jumping around on my feet and waving my arms with abandoned insecurities. I enjoyed myself, grateful to the man who got me out of the chair.

He wasn't the kind of charming that melted your heart, nor the handsome that took your breath away. What I noticed that night was his free spirit, willingness to look silly, and his wonderful rhythm.

We danced for the rest of the evening, not talking much, a few words between songs. Cursory information, nothing too personal, but interesting enough for me to take his number when he offered and give him my number when he asked. To my surprise, he called—the next day.

. . . .

OUR FIRST DATE WAS a movie. He recommended a good choice, arrived on time, and paid for the popcorn. His attire told me a lot about him—-high thread count cotton shirt with an open collar, pressed and creased khaki pants with shined and buffed penny loafers. No earrings, no necklace, no nose piercing, a modest haircut, and no obvious tattoos. His only jewelry was a leather-banded, clock-faced watch.

That was all I needed to know. He was a conservative thinker, earned an adequate income, had a decent upbringing, was secure in his appearance, and liked himself. Or, he was a con man.

I was smitten, not yet in love with him, and not the "falling in love" type. My love was my high-profile, well-paying career as a criminal lawyer. An expert consultant on high-visibility cases and a regular news commentator on matters related to criminal law. I earned success, financial security, promise of an even greater future, and incredible loneliness.

I was in no position to make a bad relationship decision. I was not willing to sacrifice my good life for a love life. But I did.

Anthony met my family; they loved him. He met my friends; they loved him. My colleagues loved him; and so did the people at church. Eventually, I guess I loved him, too.

So, we got married and lived happily ever after—or at least until he started cheating.

We were together long enough to finish each other's sentences, but not long enough to read each other's thoughts. Unfaithfulness was unexpected. Our divorce was no fault and handled quietly by a mutual friend. We kept our assets separate so there were no arguments over money. We had no children.

I never found Anthony handsome: not ugly, but not handsome. Like me, he was a lawyer, but at a four-person boutique firm specializing in tax law. He made a good but not spectacular income. He was an ok lover. I'd had better. What did other women see in him? Maybe it was his dancing.

Two years later, he remarried. A year after that, he was dead. Killed by his new wife.

. . . .

MY ASSISTANT, NANCY, came into my office and closed the door. This was unusual and made me nervous. Life was good. I wanted it to stay that way. A month before, I won a case before the Supreme Court. A lower court decision was reversed, and a man on death row, Lawrence Bollinger, released after twenty-five years of wrongful incarceration.

My face was on the cover of several publications, having just finished a full schedule of prime-time news interviews and bookings on well-rated morning shows. I was pleased with my life, but success could upend, if the media puts its eye on you. I liked media attention but was cautious.

"Lyla," Nancy said, "You're not going to want to hear this, but Anthony's widow is on the phone. She's looking for representation." Nancy shrugged. "What do you want to do?"

My ex-husband's newly widowed wife, Carol, charged with his murder, was released on bail a week before she contacted me.

After the initial news reports, media coverage was sparse. Black-on-black crime rarely stayed interesting for long.

"Move some things around. I'd like to get her in as soon as possible," I told Nancy, who appeared confused.

"OK, boss. If you say so, but you know she's going to be trouble."

I shooed Nancy out of the office. *She's right. This could be a mess, one I don't want or need.*

IT TOOK TWO DAYS TO get Carol on the schedule. Long enough for me to be sure my hair, makeup, and outfit were perfect. I am not a pretty woman; my face is all sharp angles. However, with a good make-up session, I can be attractive. I tend to be a bit chubby, but chubby can look sexy and curvy with the right outfit.

Meeting my ex-husband's widow for the first time, I wanted to shoot for stunning. I succeeded.

"You're more beautiful in person than on television," were her first words as she held out her hand for me to shake.

My office promoted confidence. I decorated it in a green and brown palette. Conservative trappings—lush forest green carpeting, wingback guest chairs covered in a pale green and brown checked plaid linen, complemented my large mahogany desk. Artwork created by African American artists adorned surfaces throughout the office. I made sure everything was sparkling in anticipation of this visit.

After Carol sat, Nancy turned on the recorder and sat on the tan leather sofa. This was our usual practice. I never liked to be alone with a client. My "maybe" client looked cautiously toward Nancy, so I said, "Carol, Nancy is my assistant and my closest confidant. I asked her to join us. She'll make a record of the meeting to supplement the tape recording. She's a certified and registered paralegal, and we have the same confidentiality rules."

Carol settled more easily into the chair, but still perched near the edge. "Ms. Williams," she began.

"No," I interrupted, "Please call me Lyla."

"Of course. Lyla, I didn't kill Tony. Somebody did, but it wasn't me."

I expected a stronger protest, something more desperate. A plea that offered a rationale for her claim of innocence or shifted the blame elsewhere. Such a simple explanation caught me off guard. This was a woman not prone to the dramatic.

"Tony left little money I can put my hands on, certainly not enough to provide me with adequate legal representation."

She keeps calling him Tony! His name was Anthony. "I'm hoping you can help with my defense. The police think they have an easy-to-prove case, but I didn't kill him. There must be some way to convince them."

I looked at the woman who probably killed my ex-husband. Much younger than Anthony, very pretty, and petite. Well dressed, not expensive, but tailored well for her body. Her nails manicured and painted with a neutral-colored polish. Hair, fashionably short with natural color. It appeared Anthony made a good choice. Unless she murdered him.

"Lyla, I can afford to pay you, but I used the house to secure my bond. I can't access Tony's insurance if I am accused of his murder."

"Then you can't afford to pay me," I retorted. Trying to intimidate and seem downright scary. I put on my best aloof expression and said, "Carol, we do a lot of pro bono work in this firm. I hope you understand. We just finished a major pro bono case that took several years, so it wouldn't be financially wise to take on another one now."

She gathered her belongings, "I understand," she said, then threw her ace on the table, "It's just, well, Tony spoke so highly of you and suggested, more than once, I should contact you if something happened to him and I needed legal guidance."

Tony, Tony, Tony, you certainly became generous with my time after you got a nickname. "Anthony was right, I'll gladly help you with a traffic ticket or his will," I said. "I don't believe he was thinking of a murder case."

I sighed and switched to my sympathetic face. "I don't know much about the case," I lied. The newspapers and court filings were my regular reading. "But I don't want Anthony's killer to escape justice. I'll have one of my associates talk to you and investigate. Once I get a better estimate of the time required, we can discuss financial arrangements."

Looking at Nancy, sitting quietly and pretending to take notes, I said, "Would you ask Quentin to come in?"

"His youth may be a surprise, Carol, but he was a great asset on the Bollinger case and I'm sure you'll be pleased with his work." *And his looks,* I thought as the gorgeous Quentin walked into my office.

Being good-looking is always an asset in contentious situations. The prettier, the better. Quentin was a major asset.

Quentin sat on the couch, well-distanced from Carol. "Quentin, this is Carol Lewis. I'm sure you've heard of the Anthony Lewis murder. Well, Anthony was Carol's husband. And, by the way, my ex-husband. Although that doesn't matter in this case."

I glanced at Quentin, whose expression screamed *This is awkward!*

"I need you to talk with Mrs. Lewis, find out what you can about her case. When you have some information, we'll help Mrs. Lewis decide how to proceed."

"Sounds great," he said with a little hesitation. "I've been looking for something to sink my teeth into since Bollinger. Thanks for the opportunity."

"Take Mrs. Lewis into the conference room for an interview. Her court date will come up soon, so we need to move quickly."

After Carol and Quentin left, Nancy turned to me and said, "I can't believe you did that."

Me neither, I shrugged.

Quentin reported back two days later. "Well, there's not much in the investigators' files beyond what's been in the papers and on TV," he told me.

"The police found Anthony on the kitchen floor with a knife in his chest. He was home alone. Carol's nightgown was in the laundry room with blood stains belonging to the victim on the front of the gown. Smudged bloody footprints led from the kitchen to the laundry room and up the stairs to the bedroom and back. She was probably wearing paper foot coverings like they use in hospitals. The authorities ransacked drawers in the bedroom. His drawers, not hers. He'd been dead for about five hours when the police arrived."

"Who called the police?" I asked.

"A neighbor across the street. She noticed the front door was wide open when she woke around 7:30. When it wasn't closed by 9, she called the police.

"The police only found one car in the three-car garage and no Carol in the house, so they went looking. They located Carol asleep in her car, parked at the neighborhood playground a few blocks away. No blood in the car or on Carol's body."

"So what's the police theory?"

"She got angry, grabbed a knife, and threw it, stabbing him. Pulled the knife from his chest. Took off her gown, threw it in the laundry room, ran up the stairs, changed clothes, somehow disposed of the knife and shoe coverings, and tried to run. The police theorize Anthony had been seeing someone else, although there is no evidence."

"She didn't get very far. What's her story?"

"Carol went to bed around midnight. Anthony hadn't come home. She took some medicine for neck pain but couldn't get to sleep and decided a drive might help her relax. She barely got out of the garage before the pain pills kicked in. She felt like she needed to pull over, and went to sleep in the car. About 10:00 a.m., she woke to the sound of police banging on the car window. They told her that her husband was dead, but disclosed 'til she got home."

"Any neighborhood cameras?"

"The neighbor across the street has one near the front door. It captures a bit of their front walkway but recorded nothing worthwhile. Their garage camera was broken. The camera at the playground caught her pulling up to the park around 4:35 a.m. He was probably dead by then."

"Any blood in the shower?"

"Nope. Blood trail stops at the laundry room door. Footprints stop at the bedroom door. Police checked all the drains, no traces of blood."

"Any motive?"

"None they can verify, so far. Carol says they weren't having problems, money or otherwise. Anthony often worked past midnight, so she wasn't surprised when he hadn't come home. The record of the burglar alarm at his office confirms his late hours. She says she didn't hear him come in.

"The police haven't found a motive, either. They think she just got mad because he kept coming home so late."

"What do you think?"

"I agree with the police," Quentin said. "I think she did it."

. . . .

ONE THING I LIKED ABOUT Quentin was, like me, he was pragmatic. In a case like this, it's usually the spouse. He said, "I know it's not my place, but why would you want to get involved in this? It's pretty open and shut, and well below the radar.

"Once you're involved, your history with the victim gets exposed, and the media will be all over the place. It's really a case anybody could handle.

"There are a few open questions, but not enough to change the basic facts. He came home late. Not an unusual reason for anger. Enraged, she stabbed him. Then, in a panic, she ran away. Simple.

"She'll get some time for manslaughter, probably not a lot. She can be out in five or six years.."

He was right, of course. "But if she's innocent, why jail time at all?"

"Lyla, this doesn't sound like you. Is there anything else I should know?"

"Not really," I answered. "Who's the detective?"

"Millicent Carl. Not senior, assigned to a few other cases. This is her first murder."

"Is she working alone?"

"No. Jack Gerard is also on the case. But, he's planning to retire soon and seldom shows up in the office these days."

"Good. Let's see what Ms. Carl and Mr. Gerard have to say."

Quentin knitted his brow. "You want to call Millicent?"

"No, I want you to. I'll listen. She shouldn't talk to us, but maybe she's not too bright."

To be honest, I went to law school with Millicent Carl's father. He had the brains of a corncob. His daughter is likely a cloned kernel.

• • • •

"DETECTIVE MILLICENT Carl," is how she answered Quentin's call.

"Hi, Detective Carl. This is Quentin James from the Williams and Williams Law Firm." He was on speakerphone, so I could listen in the background. I could imagine Millicent sitting straighter in her chair at the mention of his name and the firm. I couldn't tell whether she was responding to the name of the law firm or Quentin's name. Rumors of Quentin's long eyelashes often outweighed his need for credibility.

"I need to talk to you about the Carol Lewis case," he said.

"Of course," she replied. *No, Millicent, you're supposed to refer him to the District Attorney. Yep, not too bright.*

Quentin looked at me and smirked. "I've been reviewing the detective files on the case. We may represent her. Have you gotten any new information since the bail hearing?"

We could hear papers being moved around on her desk. "Looking at my file, we have done little more. We went back to look for the murder weapon. No luck. The coroner is sure it was a kitchen butcher knife. There was one missing from the kitchen drawers. We also looked for blood on the shoes she was wearing. Clean. We checked all the shoes in her closet. No luck there, either. We think she had coverings on her shoes. The DA thinks we have enough information to indict her for manslaughter, but the foot coverings indicate some premeditation, so they may give it another go," Quentin said.

"Anything on motive?"

"Not yet. Their finances appear in good shape. We couldn't find her husband involved with another woman. Or man. Of course, he was coming in late a lot, but it's tax season. Neither have any reported mental health issues." I could hear her common sense kick in as her voice got firmer. "I probably shouldn't be talking to you this much. From now on, contact Ashley Phillips. She's the DA assigned to the Lewis case."

"Of course I will, Millicent. Thanks for your help." Click, call over.

Quentin and I shared a smile.

• • • •

ASHLEY PHILLIPS' BRIGHT makeup entered the room before she did. Quentin would later say he could see the bright purple lipstick, matching eyeshadow, and blush with its gold highlights from two blocks away. Her personality matched her make-up. She marched to our table. "It might have been a mistake to invite me to this here fancy restaurant," she boomed in an accent sounding like Missouri bootheel.

A little out of place here in the City. "You cain't bribe me with no steak and potatoes." She glanced around the sunny room. "Or quiche and salad."

Quentin raised his eyebrows and stood to hold her chair while saying, "I hope you didn't think we planned to pay for your meal. You eat, you pay. It's been a rule of this firm for years. Ask anybody."

"You don't want to be here? We can go to your dreary, musty office. Or we can go to the monkey house at the zoo. Your choice."

Quentin seemed about to go on a roll of insults, but I interrupted. "Please sit down, Ms. Phillips." She flopped in the chair; it squeaked in protest. The woman's appearance screamed poor eating habits, lack of home training, no cultural experience, and online law school. *She must be pretty smart to work in the DA's office.* I looked at Quentin. *Don't underestimate her,* I was thinking. I could tell he'd come to the same conclusion.

"I'm surprised to see you here, Ms. Williams, or should I say, Mrs. Lewis." She had done some homework. I was careful not to exchange a glance with my associate.

"I wasn't even Mrs. Lewis when I was married to Anthony," I responded. "Don't call me that, very few people will know who you're talking about, and I might not respond."

"Well, Ms. Whatever You Call Yourself, our detective shouldn't have spoken to you. I'm here to get us on the right track."

"No, you're here because you're curious to meet me. And because this is a nice restaurant." I was well into my aloof attitude. "So, let me set you straight. We are representing Mrs. Lewis in this case, and we're preparing for her indictment hearing. I understand it's scheduled for a few weeks. July 10th?" Ashley nodded. "Please understand, Ms. Phillips, our client is innocent." I let her absorb my statement, not respond.

Continuing, I said, "Mr. James is the lead on the case, but you can expect to see me from time to time. All your contact will be through

Mr. James. You won't get a response if you try to contact me directly. If you try more than once, you can expect a reprimand from your boss."

I finished my glass of water, placed my napkin on the table. And said. "I'm tired of this conversation. Quentin, come to see me when you return to the office."

· · · ·

HE RETURNED A COUPLE of hours later. "Nancy's going to the DA's office to pick up a copy of the case file. Ashley wants to bargain from first-degree murder down to manslaughter. Ten to twenty years. She's basing the first degree on the foot coverings."

"Then she's insane as well as tacky." I would have said ugly, but who could tell under that makeup?

"Who kills somebody in their nightgown, takes the time to cover their feet, then simply throws the blood-stained nightgown in the laundry room? Where are those foot coverings? Where is the blood on her? I think we should request dismissal due to a lack of evidence. There's not enough to arrest her, much less bring murder charges."

"I agree, but Ashley seemed pretty adamant. Maybe there's something surprising in the files."

· · · ·

SURPRISING WAS AN UNDERSTATEMENT.

I was in my apartment kitchen drinking coffee, quite pleased with myself. The scroll under the mock serious-looking faces of the morning show anchors read, "Noted attorney Lyla Williams has agreed to defend the wife of her murdered ex-husband, Tony Lewis. The authorities suspect his new wife of the murder." *I loved hearing my name on the news.*

The phone rang. It was my building's front desk attendant. Quentin and Nancy wanted to come up. *Both of them? It's not even eight o'clock!*

I couldn't read their faces, but they looked tired. They immediately loaded file folders onto my kitchen table.

"We spent most of last night and this morning reviewing the files we got from the DA's office," Quentin said. "There are some surprises, some shocks, and then there are some things beyond anything you could imagine."

He looked at Nancy. "Where should we start?"

"Let's work our way up," she replied.

Nancy continued. "First, Anthony and Carol were in some kind of financial scheme. They kept a joint bank account and one under only Carol's maiden name. Carol's account was hiding the problems. It looks like they were moving unusual amounts of money in and out of the account on a regular basis. At one point, the Carol account was flush with money. A few days later it was at zero. Then, there was an untraceable, large infusion of cash, around $150,000 into the Carol account, and everything was stable again. For about a year."

"Then, things hit bottom again," Quentin said. "This time, there were a few large deposits, around $25,000 and unexplained withdrawals averaging $5,000 a week from the Carol account. Most months, the joint bank account had close to zero balance."

I said, "Anthony made little more than $15,000 in a month. And Carol is what? A secretary? Were they playing in some sort of get rich quick scheme?"

Nancy replied, "I know, right? Almost all of his money went into her account. Hold on, there's more."

Quentin continued, "About six months ago, they each took out an insurance policy. Five hundred thousand dollars for each of them. One policy is payable to the holder of the other.

"They were term policies, not very expensive to get into, but given their financial condition, a sign they were looking out for each other in case one of them might not live long."

l placed my hands on the edge of my seat, ready for another bombshell.

Nancy took over the narrative. "Mrs. Carol Lewis is not the virtuous woman we thought she was."

"Well, we all have some skeletons," I said.

"Yes, we do," Nancy agreed. "Carol Lewis, nee Walker, was a call girl before Anthony. Sexy pictures online."

I didn't completely fall off my chair, but it tilted.

"How could the police miss that?"

"Well, they didn't. Millicent did. The site was in one of those secret web places. I expect Detective Gerard found it. Millicent is too naïve to even think that way."

"Naïve is not the word," I said.

"The pictures got filthier over time," Quentin added in a tone that sounded to me like he was sad but being sarcastic.

"This is too serious for jokes," I admonished.

"He's not joking," Nancy interjected. "They're bad. Or good, depending on your point of view. But it's all beside the point.

"Millicent didn't seem to know any of this and I'm sure she has no reason to conceal this kind of smut."

"Right," responded Quentin. "Maybe it's time to talk to Detective Gerard."

· · · ·

DETECTIVE JACK GERARD was an old friend of my family. He and Dad had been drinking buddies back in the day, and I think he dated my mother when they were teenagers. Like any city, the black community was a spiderweb of connections. Usually, if you don't know the individual, you know someone in the family or a close friend.

In his late sixties, Jack was still a handsome man. A regular visitor to the gym, he kept his wardrobe up-to-date and his ancestors blessed him with good skin and a full head of now white hair.

We met at my dad's favorite bar. Jack was sitting in a booth nursing a shot glass full of brown liquid. He started shaking his head as I sat down. "Lolly, what have you gotten yourself into? Has your daddy called yet? I'm sure he has a few words for you." Only a few people remembered my childhood nickname. The man sitting across from me was one of two people in the world I still allowed to call me by it. The other person was my father.

"Are you hiding from the press yet?" he asked. "If I were you I'd go incognito, now. By tomorrow, this will move from a minor news story to Entertainment Tonight."

"I guess I wasn't thinking straight, Uncle Jack. I know I should have called you first."

"Wait a minute, Baby. This is not your daddy here. This is your Uncle Jack. Don't forget, I have inside knowledge of the mysteries underneath those well-coiffed curls of yours."

He laughed. "You always think straight, always calculating. Well, with the one exception, we will never discuss.

"You know I never cared for your ex. Too soft. I was happy when you got rid of him. And, since I think you were happy to get rid of him, too, why are you getting wrapped up in this mess? You can't be low on clients."

I avoided his eyes. I could stand up to all kinds of powerful people, including my father. But my Uncle Jack? He could see right through me. "It was an opportunity for publicity. I have a book coming out early next year and thought this might give me a chance to keep my name out there a while longer. At first glance, it seemed simple. She killed him but there isn't enough evidence to prove it."

I buried my face in my hands, then said, "I thought I could get the case dismissed and ride on a wave of glory. I'd have saved her from a murder charge."

"That's mostly a lie. You know it. So do I. But let's move on. I guess you want to know what I've found out besides what's in the files."

"Yes, please. It's obvious you don't trust your partner, Detective Millicent."

"Sweet Millicent has a lot to learn. Like how to keep her mouth closed. But she's one of the smartest people on the police force. She's shy." He pulled a small notebook from his jacket pocket. "Ashley is almost as smart as you and anything but shy. Note, I said almost. Her appearance, like yours, is an act. She's a better actress than you. Never trust her."

Uncle Jack seemed perturbed, so I said, "I didn't bother you because I thought this was simple. It's not. As soon as I realized, I came right here."

"Sure, now do like I tell you. You got yourself in this and dropping it at this point would hurt your client and your reputation.

"I know you've turned the case over to that associate you seem to like so much. What is his name? Quincy? You need to go through the files yourself. Everything I hear, he's really smart, but this is not the kind of thing you turn over to an associate. There are personal things you need to watch out for. Things only you would notice."

"His name is Quentin, and I'll start right away."

"Given some of my theories, 'right away' is not soon enough. Get back to me when you're done."

He slid out of the booth and stopped. "Is there any reason you and Quentin seem so close? Is he your new boyfriend? He's young." My Uncle Jack laughed.

● ● ● ●

OF COURSE, UNCLE JACK was right about the case files.

I started with the crime scene photos Nancy had loaded on my computer. My first discovery: There was a butcher knlife missing from the set in the kitchen. The police thought it was the murder weapon. Only I could tell the knife used to kill Anthony was not from the set in the kitchen. I left the house, all its contents, and him when we separated. Good riddance. I didn't take anything but my clothes and cosmetics. But I remembered all the luxuries that were once mine.

Our appliances and kitchenware were high end. The picture in the case file was a catalog picture of the knife the coroner speculated as a murder weapon. It would fit the set in the kitchen drawer, but as I remembered the sensual feel of the expensive knife handles against my palm, I could tell the coroner wrongly identified the weapon. Even a high end, super sharp, kitchen butcher knife couldn't do this. Also, Anthony wasn't stabbed by someone standing close to him.

The knife had penetrated at a perfect 90-degree angle. If the not-too-tall, small-boned Carol had stabbed him in the course of an argument, it should have tilted upwards. The murderer must have thrown the knife . Thrown it with enough strength to cut through Anthony's sweater, into his man boobs, through his rib cage, straight into his heart. This was the work of someone you didn't want to challenge in darts.

The detectives had rifled through Anthony's home office drawers. The pictures showed a mess of paper and binders. It was in the mess that I made my second discovery: Something no one would notice but me.

· · · ·

WHEN ANTHONY AND I divorced, we closed all our accounts and divided the proceeds. The divorce happened over five years ago. Yet, the picture showed his desk, under a messy pile of papers, a voided blank check from a local credit union. I could see the credit union's name and a portion of the account number. I enlarged my computer screen to better see the numbers. The voided check with no visible name, amount, or signature, was from an account I used when I was single. I thought it was closed, yet the date on the check was a month before Anthony's murder.

If the account was active, I was the sole signatory.

I called the bank. Surprisingly, the password hadn't changed after all these years. The account had a balance of over twenty million dollars.

. . . .

I WASN'T SURE WHAT to do with this new information. I was too embarrassed to tell Uncle Jack. But I had to tell Nancy.

We were sitting in a dimly lit establishment named Dive Bar drinking Jack Daniels on the rocks. The bar had the musty/sweet smell left by decades of alcoholic drinks, sweaty bodies, and cigarettes. Known for its heavy pours of hard liquor, it stayed busy. The Dive Bar was not a place to find a good Chardonnay or fancy cocktails. None of my chichi friends would be around, and I was unlikely to be recognized by the other customers.

"Twenty million three hundred twenty-six dollars and forty cents," Nancy said. She'd followed up on my call to the bank. No transactions in the past six months. "We'll have to go deeper into the account for more information. Given the amount of money involved, our inquiries would cause questions."

"What about taxes?" I wondered aloud.

Nancy, seated across from me in a booth upholstered in forty-year-old orange pleather, grabbed my hand and said, "I can't imagine how it got deposited into the account without IRS suspicion, but if you haven't accounted for the money on a tax return, tax evasion charges may be in you future."

Nancy was my one true ride-or-die. We stayed best friends since grade school. I loved her, but right then, I wanted to punch her in the nose.

"Why would you say that, Nancy? I'm nervous enough."

"Because it's true and because you may need a lawyer of your own. You're in trouble, my friend."

THE LATE ANTHONY HAD been the best tax attorney locally, so I called his mentor, Gary Gray, while still at the bar. Gary was a well-known tax attorney based in Chicago.

He returned my call within minutes. I slid down in the seat and tried to engage in conversation over the pulsating blues recording playing in the background. Nancy listened.

Known as the tax attorney to the stars, Gary wasn't one for pleasantries. "I saw on the news that you are defending your ex's wife charged with his murder. That's some stupid stuff. Now I'm getting a call from you. I have a feeling you have done something even more stupid than I thought."

I didn't go into all the details, but I let him know my dead ex-husband had been using an old checking account still bearing my name. Only my name. When I told him the account balance, he said, "You gotta be kidding", so loud that Nancy heard him over the music.

"No, Gary, no kidding here. I know absolutely nothing about this money, where it came from, or how it found its way to this account. I thought the account had been closed years ago before I was married."

"Does your client know about the money?"

"I haven't asked her yet. There are also some strange things going onwith her and Anthony's accounts. I need to decide on a strategy."

"Well, assume the police already know about the money. They just haven't told you. Also, if you didn't leak the information about your representation of Mrs. Lewis, you can assume someone from the police did, or maybe your client did.

"You should also assume the leaker will continue to leak, has a grudge against you, and would like nothing more than to see you under pressure. Or on trial. Or in jail."

Gary took a breath. "I guess you called for my advice, so here it is. Print off copies of the bank statements and your tax returns for at least six years before your divorce to the present. Get a lawyer to take them to the police and call the IRS. You should assume this is dirty money and you're going to need to get away from it as soon as you can."

He continued. "Judging from the music in the background, you're sitting in the dark, some place drinking away your problems. It won't work. Finish your drink and hurry. You want to be on the offensive.

"That's my last free advice. Anything else will cost. A lot. You have enough money in the bank to pay me," he laughed at his joke. It wasn't a joke to me. End of conversation.

. . . .

NANCY HELPED ME WITH the bank statements while I gathered the taxes. Rather than turn them over to the DA, I called Uncle Jack the lead detective. I'd made my mind up to hire Gary as my interface with the IRS. Uncle Jack seemed pleased by my call. We arranged to meet at the same watering hole as before.

"Looks like drugs to me," he said while sipping his drink. "Or, most likely, human trafficking, given your client's side job. By the way, when do you confront her? I hope it's right after you leave here. I can't wait to hear what she has to say. Gotta be the best piece of fiction created since Sherlock Holmes.

"Don't mention this to Millicent or Ashley. The DA already has a lot of information. Don't risk giving them more than they need. Going to the IRS is all you need to cover your ass."

"What is all this about, Uncle Jack?" I felt like a little girl asking for a present. "A week ago, I was riding high on my accomplishments. Today I'm trying to stave off federal prison. What do you think is happening?"

"Well, first, I'm sure your client is guilty. I am not yet sure she is guilty of murdering her husband, but she sure as hell is guilty of something—something bad. Your dead ex-husband, too. Although, he didn't seem smart enough to pull off major crimes."

Jack took a long breath, as if he were preparing for a major speech. "Let me give you a little background you should have gotten before you married Anthony. First off, he liked to say his parents were dead and he avoided the rest of his family because they would bring him down. Them being on welfare and everything.

"Baby girl, ain't no black person in this country who doesn't have some kinda family they're close to, no matter how bad the people are. Right off, your father and I saw a red flag and looked into him.

"You know he's from the islands. The land of laid-back living and rum punch. It's also sometimes known for drugs and underage pimping. Your former honey's family was heavily into underage kiddies. His mother was being pimped when she got knocked up with him. His father pulled her out of the business at about fourteen or so. She'd been in the business since she was ten."

"WHAT? Is she still alive?"

"Oh, yeah. A magnificent woman. Jaw-dropping beautiful. Think Lena Horne. Your Daddy could hardly stop looking at her."

"You visited her?"

"Of course. Any excuse for drinking rum on the beach," he motioned for the bartender to bring another drink. "Plus, as sooThey named the main character Tony.

n as we learned his real name, we thought he needed some first-hand snooping."

"His real name?"

"Yep, you married and divorced Tony Jardin Louis. Not Anthony, Tony. Not Lewis, Louis." he gave me a minute to catch my breath.

"Brothers? Sisters?"

"Yep, a slew of them. Two sisters from his mother and a bunch of sisters and brothers from his Daddy."

"His Daddy?"

"Yeah, think for a minute. You've heard of Thibault Louis."

I had. Thibault Louis, or Teddy as he liked to be called, was notorious: accused of more vicious crimes than anyone could keep track of but never tried for any of them. There was a Netflix series based on his life; it was called *Horrendous*. They called the main character Tony.

Suddenly, the taxes seemed like a minor problem.

Uncle Jack continued, "We didn't speak to Teddy, but Anthony's mother was happy about his marriage to you.

"Gigi, his mother's name, was sad not to be invited to the wedding, but she understood it was best to stay in the background. I remember her saying, 'Tony has a good life, a good education, and now a good woman. We have developed a background for him that will be very difficult to penetrate. We plan to leave him alone. He's a good boy and has no stomach for this business. Someday, the family may need him, but I hope it's never. I am pretty sure it will never be. Tony has plenty of very smart sisters and brothers, some of whom are already lawyers. We will be unknown to Lyla unless you want otherwise.'

"After our meeting, your Dad and I thought it was ok for you to get married and to go along with the family's wishes not to tell you. Anthony promised he'd tell you himself one day. But then you divorced and now he's dead." Uncle Jack shrugged as if to say, "C'est la vie."

He finished his drink and prepared to leave. "The DA has figured none of this out, so do not spread it around. Don't even tell your pet, Quentin.

"One last thing, and I don't think anybody outside Anthony's family knows this little tidbit. Carol is Anthony's sister."

• • • • •

I CALLED MY FATHER, "Uncle Jack talked to you?" were the first words from my mouth.

"Sure did. We discussed everything. I think you should drop all this like a hot potato and come down to Florida and visit me for a while.

This stuff will get nasty. Your case will go from a scroll across the screen to words read from a teleprompter in a matter of hours. Somebody is feeding the press information.

"Jack and I disagree on the source. I think it's the DA. I'm sure she's jealous. Jack thinks it's deeper, more nefarious. Come on, Sweetie, visit your Daddy. Get out of town."

"No, I need to stay here, take care of my business."

"Well, call me. Let me know what's happening." He sounded sad.

I said "bye" to my father and went to visit Carol.

• • • •

I MET CAROL AT HER house, which was once my house. Nothing much had changed. It just looked a little more dingy than I remembered. She offered me coffee, tea, or wine. If she'd offered Jack Daniels, I might have accepted. This was going to be an awkward conversation. I was nervous for the first time in a long time, although I refused to let it show.

"I'll just take water, Carol. This may take a while." She returned with a plastic bottle of water, no glass. I wondered why she wasn't using the expensive water filtration system Anthony installed when we were married.

"I am still a little uncomfortable going into the kitchen," she said while settling in one of the rose-pink slipper chairs across from the dark blue contemporary sofa where I sat. I looked down at the handwoven area rug and considered asking for a glass of red wine just so I could pour it over the furniture. It still felt like mine.

"I understand how you can feel uncomfortable, but we have many more uncomfortable subjects to broach today," I said.

"First, how did you learn to throw a knife? That kind of skill doesn't come easy."

Her puzzled expression, clearly said, "Huh?" Her voice said, "I don't understand." She started crossing and uncrossing her legs.

I'd thrown her composure off, so I kept going. "Anthony wasn't killed the way the police think. The entry wound isn't right. We can come back around to the knife."

"You and Anthony had some funny business going on with your finances. And, where did you get the millions in the bank account you kept under my name?" Her mouth dropped open so fast she almost drooled.

"Carol, are you a full-time or part-time hooker?

"Is incest common in your family? Or was this one of those special loves?"

Her spine straight, she stood up, tossed her hair, and left the room. I could hear her walking upstairs toward the bedroom.

I wanted to check the kitchen and took this opportunity to do so. It was spotless. No one in this house cooked. The kitchen looked like untouched since Anthony and I remodeled when we first moved in. I didn't cook either.

I checked the drawers. Everything was in its place except for the knives. The knives were in their slots except one - the supposed murder weapon.

I tried to remember the crime scene photos. Anthony's body was on its side, crunched in a fetal position, between the kitchen island and the stove. He'd probably stood with his back against the stove. When the knife hit him, he crumpled to the floor in an awkward position. There wasn't a lot of space for him to fall.

There was no sign that he tried to grab the knife or brace himself on the counter before falling. It must've happened fast. He likely didn't quite realize what happened until he reached the floor. The pictures showed evidence of him touching the floor and bottom trim of the kitchen island as he died. Footprints stepped over the body, took the knife, stopped by the laundry room, and went upstairs.

I wondered why Anthony was standing in the seldom-used kitchen.

I KINDA EXPECTED CAROL to return with a gun or a knife. Instead, she came with tears, snot, and a box of tissues.

"I guess you called home," I said.

She nodded and blew her nose. She was having a really ugly cry. All of her composure was gone.

"I guess, given the direction of your questions, you know about our family."

Was this a threat? I answered cautiously, "Yes I've been told a bit of your family background."

"Well, my mother thinks one of the other family lawyers should come here to work with you," she dabbed her face, leaving specks of tissue on her cheeks and nose.

"It's not that she doesn't trust you. We've all been proud of you and have admired your successes. You are so smart. But, if the family business is going to be exposed, you are going to need help with understanding how things work and how to deal with the press."

OMG. I am a member of a mob family.

. . . .

THE FAMILY REPRESENTATIVE called me later that evening and asked or maybe told me to meet their lawyer for lunch at a restaurant about an hour and a half away. I was too curious to refuse.

I was tired when I arrived. I spent the night binging *Horrendous*. Just nervous before, the TV show scared the bejesus out of me. Walking into the restaurant, dragging my feet, I knew I looked like I felt–a sad, old broken car.

We met in one of the most popular restaurants in the country. Recently featured in the NYT food section, it usually took months to get a reservation but the Thibault family made it happen overnight. It's all in who you threaten, or so they say.

As you may have guessed by now, I'm a sucker for a good-looking man. Jean Rene Louis certainly checked the "WOW" box. He was wearing blue jeans and a hoodie with what looked to be a wrinkled T-shirt underneath. His shoes were generic Nikes. For sure, he didn't want to be mistaken for a lawyer or someone with money. Even his fingernails, though clean, were ragged. He flashed a smile of perfectly veneered teeth against his chocolate skin.

Who were these people? Oh, yeah, the scum of the earth.

"Hello, Ms. Williams. I'm Jean Rene Louis," he said as he joined me at the table. "You're prettier than your pictures. I'm Tony and Carol's cousin. The son of their grandfather," he said, again flashing that flawless smile.

He looked close to Quentin's age. I narrowed my eyes, looked more closely. He said, "I was a late-life surprise, but I have two younger sisters. My Daddy likes surprises."

After ordering the largest hamburger on the menu, he said, "I'm licensed to practice in almost every state in the US. I intentionally skipped some of the southern states. I hate being angry about history." He spoke his words with the wonderful lyrical cadence often heard in the voice of islanders.

He continued, "I, too, am a criminal lawyer. I'm quite smart, like your associate, Quentin James, but my experience is not as strong. I hope to learn a lot from you both. The whole family is pleased I have this opportunity. We all admire you."

"I hope to learn from you, too." I said, "Specifically, I'm hoping you have the information to explain this confusing puzzle."

"Well, I can explain some things, but others we will have to find out together," he said

. . . . .

"LET ME START BY APOLOGIZING for all of us," Jean-Rene said. "My family thought this was something easily handled. Does someone want to make it a major news story? We never should have involved you. However, your relationship with Tony would have been mentioned, eventually."

His eyes focused on mine with an intense stare. "We keep the family connection hidden for Tony's sake." He wanted a normal life. His fake birth certificate, education records, and former mailing addresses protected his identity. Even his childhood inoculation records are invented.

"But someone has killed him and that someone is working hard to frame Carol and tie his murder to our business."

"Why do you think she is being framed? Why don't you at least consider her guilty?"

"Because she is Tony's sister and our family doesn't murder people. This would hurt the family reputation. She loved her brother without boundaries."

"Your family approved of their relationship?"

"Oh yes. Their mother suggested it." He stalled before saying, "But it's not like you think. After you and Tony divorced, everyone was concerned about him. He was irresponsible when he was single, before he married you and no one wanted him to fall back into those bad habits. So, who better to keep tabs on him than his sister? It was their idea to say they were married. I don't know why."

Ok. Enough bullshit.

"Jean Rene," I said, "let's talk about the money."

"Of course. My cousin, Teddy, described in popular culture as a devil, is said to be engaged in drugs, prostitution, and human trafficking. That is not the truth." His face looked sad. "Early in his career, he was involved with some terrible people who were, not to his knowledge, involved in the nasty business. He invested their money.

"When he found out, he wanted to be sure no more of this activity involved his family, but there was a price. Every once in a while, they asked him to do some financial work for them. Tony would sometimes handle that work.

"It was very discreet, and Tony's fingerprints aren't on the transactions. Except for this once. Some money needed to be put aside for safekeeping. Your bank account has been keeping it safe."

He reached across the table to lay a consoling hand on mine. Looking at me with starry brown eyes, he said, "The money traces to a legal real estate transaction. A few years ago, Tony sold a small but profitable hotel on the Island of Freeport."

"What? He owned a hotel?"

"Ms. Williams, may I call you Lyla?" I nodded yes. I was too overwhelmed to object. He continued, "There was no hotel. But the sale appears completely legitimate. I handled the paperwork myself.

"Please understand that your former father-in-law is a legitimate investment banker. Probably one of the most successful in the world. Many mainstream billion-dollar start-ups exist because of his leadership." *Yeah, and Vito Corleone sold olive oil.*

"He has to keep his business dealings hidden because of the negative reputation assigned to him by others. But even legitimate businesses sometimes have to do shady things. We're sorry you got involved."

· · · ·

GROWING UP, I WASN'T the pretty girl, not even cute. I wasn't the athletic girl. I dreaded athletic activities. I was the smart girl. Being the smart girl means never really fitting in with the popular folks. So, my intelligence pushed me forward in life, but away from the crowd. To cope, I developed an alternative persona to stand in when I need to appear more self-confident. I called her Linda.

When I left the meeting with Jean Rene, Linda went on vacation. I drove home feeling I needed a friend to take Linda's place. A few years ago, that friend would be Anthony. The man who got me to stand up and dance would be home waiting for me. Sometimes, when he knew I had a rough day, he would go to the movie theater to get popcorn—layered with butter. He would add hot dogs to the order. When I got home, he would have my favorite feast waiting with a bottle of chilled champagne. We didn't need glasses, we'd chug it right from the bottle and wipe our greasy, sticky mouths with our hands. After a while, we would have laughed the bad day away.

In the last ten days, my Anthony became the Tony person. A stranger. The Tony person deceived me, shared my secrets, told others my weaknesses.

Only my Anthony knew how I liked to be complimented on my appearance. He often teased me about liking my professional ego stroked. He would have suggested they choose a Michelin-rated restaurant to impress me. He would be the one to suggest my contact be good-looking.

This Tony person violated secrets I once thought were especially ours. He put me at criminal risk and tried to destroy my reputation. Yet at this moment, for the first time since his death, I missed him.

• • • •

I SAT IN MY CAR HAVING a pity party for at least a half-hour before I went to my apartment. My Daddy and Uncle Jack were waiting inside.

Daddy looked horrified. I'd been crying. I felt my make-up smeared over my face, my hair into who knows what kind of look, and I was holding my shoes. I don't think he'd seen me cry since I was five.

"What the fuck?" he exclaimed. "Did somebody die? Your brother? Your sister? One of your nieces?"

I whimpered, "No."

Uncle Jack said simply, "Go get yourself together and come back. We need to talk."

I was my dad's favorite. My sister, the artist, was a nice girl but wasting her life. My brother, a very successful lawyer, lived in Los Angeles. He was gay. To Daddy, he lived on a faraway planet, but not far enough away. His hopes and dreams rested with the pitiful woman standing in front of him, crying.

I washed my face, combed my hair, and changed into blue jeans and a tee shirt. I put on a little make-up so Daddy would see I still had some pride.

"So what happened?" Uncle Jack asked.

"I took your advice and went to see Carol. She confessed her innocence again as well as more tears and snot than you can imagine. She called her mother, who sent a family lawyer to help out. He arrived today. I met him for lunch."

"Who did they send?" my father asked.

"A young lawyer, Jean-Rene Louis. He is the son of Tony and Carol's grandfather."

"Gabriel," my father said. "What upsetting nonsense did this Jean-Rene Louis say?"

I went through the conversation. Tony's fake background, their mother's decision to send Carol to Tony, the money-laundering scheme, and Tony's good business sense. I mentioned their long-time admiration of my work and ended my summary by saying, "Daddy, Uncle Jack, Anthony played me. Royally played me, and I don't know for how long. Probably more than a decade."

I felt my self-confidence returning. "But it all stops. Right here, right now." I was ready to kick ass. "So what do you two gentlemen know? What haven't you told me?"

My father stood up. He was once a very handsome man, known for his ability to charm an adversary. But years of physical neglect resulted in this tired old man standing in my living room now looking like a scared child. Daddy said, "I need to confess.

"I've known of their interest in you for some time." He paced. I'd learned a long time ago that his pacing meant he was about to drop a hammer. "Gigi and I talk from time to time. She thought you might be interested in doing some business with the family."

Uncle Jack jumped from his chair and grabbed his shoulders, his abs to Daddy's flab, and practically spitting in his face, yelled, "Fuck you! Have you been talking to that woman about your daughter becoming a criminal? Your daughter?"

Uncle Jack fell back on the sofa and said, "Man, you as old as dirt and have cataracts on both eyes, but you still can't resist a pretty face. Lordy, me! When does it end!"

My father looked crushed. "I thought I was helping, Jack. Helping them keep Lyla away from their criminal activities. I told Gigi the request to get my daughter involved in their activities was out of the question."

I went to my bar and poured three large Jack Daniels. "Gentlemen, let's talk."

• • • •

MY APARTMENT IS SPARE. Think Scandinavian design. The spirit of the cold weather Caucasian population dominated: squared corner edges and monochromatic. The gray, tan, and white pallet calmed Uncle Jack and my father. I gave them a minute to sip their drinks before starting my interrogation. "First question: how much do you two know about this subterfuge underlying my life?"

Uncle Jack answered first. "As I told you the other day, I found out about Anthony when you told us you were going to marry him. Back then, it wasn't hard to find his identity was false. A double-check with the hospital where he was supposedly born, a check for his non-existent elementary and high school records. His college records and past job references were valid, so we didn't think he was a criminal. We just

knew something was off."

Uncle Jack was slowly sipping his drink. Daddy drained the glass and poured himself a refill.

Uncle Jack continued, "The next step was harder. We needed to find out who he was. We took several pictures of him and put them through the FBI database, where we located his original passport. Issued when he was 17 years old."

"Nobody can do a similar search on him now," my father interjected. "After we found him, the family shut all holes in his fake identity.

"A friend living in the islands got in touch with Gigi. She was easy to find and, on the surface, living a crime-free life.

"Delighted to see us, she explained the family was very high profile and not in a good way. Tony, she explained, was not connected to the family business and didn't want to be. She said Tony didn't want to live with the media, FBI, and others always looking over his shoulder."

Daddy went on. "Of course, she investigated your background. Gigi is very protective. She was excited he was marrying into such a reputable family, and you seemed primed to continue our family's stellar reputation.

"In short, she thought it was very good for him to marry you. There would be no pushback from the family. No support, either. Their deal with Anthony was he make it on his own. She begged us not to tell you. It was important that Anthony keep his life separate.

"She kept direct contact with Anthony to a minimum. She called me maybe once or twice a year. Nothing serious. Mostly about the possibility of grandchildren."

"When's the last time you talked?"

"Right before you and Anthony split. She was worried about you both and didn't understand the circumstances. Neither did I."

"She didn't call you when he died?"

"She called me," Uncle Jack answered. "Wanted to know what I knew. I didn't know anything, then.

"I got myself assigned to his murder case and browsed through the case files. A guy in the squad room suggested I look at this escort website. It's where I found Carol. The guy recognized her from a case several years back. She was only about 19 then and, like many other girls was an escort for extra money while in college. I pulled up the arrest record and found out her real last name was Louis and Tony Louis posted her bond. Checking websites devoted to the Louis family, I found an old picture of Carol as a child with her big brother, Tony. If I didn't know them, I wouldn't have put two and two together. They don't look very much alike."

My father asked, "Have you shared what you know with Gigi?"

"No, and don't you!" Uncle Jack exclaimed.

I said, "Carol is still my client. My job is to defend her on the murder charge. I don't know how this pieces together, but tomorrow, I work on her defense and her defense only. Hopefully, everything will fall into place."

Daddy and Uncle Jack left. Daddy could hardly stand upright. I looked at the almost empty liquor bottle and shook my head, worried about his health.

• • • •

EXHAUSTED, I POURED myself one more small drink and went to bed. Sleep came a few minutes at a time. If it weren't for my restlessness, I probably wouldn't have heard the commotion in the living room.

Whoever it was didn't try to be quiet. I could hear movement sounding like things being shifted around. I didn't have a gun and only dreamed about knowing martial arts. Confronting the intruder seemed like a bad idea. I reached for my cell phone and found it hadn't charged. The battery was dead.

I could hear footsteps on the floor of the white marble-tiled hallway leading to my room. I rushed to lock the door and pull a chair under the doorknob. Next, I crawled under the bed and covered my ears.

Someone tried the doorknob, then pushed hard on the door. My response was to yell, "Go away or I'll shoot," as loud as I could.

A male voice laughed. His footsteps retreated down the hall. I heard the front door open and close.

My phone was on the nightstand next to the bed with the charger attached but not plugged into the wall. My exhausted mind forgot the key step. I scrambled to plug it up. It took a few minutes for the phone to locate a signal.

The police arrived 10 minutes after I called to report an intruder. The front desk attendant let them in.

I ran to greet them and found my neutral-colored living room covered in what looked to be blood. The deep red color splashed on my walls, smeared on my furniture, and tracked on my carpet. Bloody footsteps led to my bedroom door. The police searched the entire house. There was no source for the blood, but a butcher knife lay on my kitchen counter.

The police questioned me for what seemed like hours. I had no explanation for the knife, the blood, the voice--nothing. Not a single thing stolen, only a couple of lamps broken and pictures pulled from the walls. It looked like someone was trying to scare me. Maybe a disgruntled client? The only problem was the knife.

The police brought in their forensics team and quickly determined the stuff resembling blood was water-based paint. The knife was bagged and sent to the police lab for analysis.

Detective Millicent arrived as the officers, and forensics team were finishing their work. There was no place for both of us to sit. I in the one chair not covered with paint and I wasn't going to offer it to her. She stood awkwardly in the middle of the floor, looking like she knew she should ask questions, but what questions? As expected, she asked the most obvious, "Ms. Williams, who do you think made this mess?"

"Beats me."

Next stupid question, "Could it have been you?"

"Why would I trash the place I live in?"

"To cover up something?"

"Cover-up what?"

Millicent was getting uncomfortable, standing in front of me in her serviceable, low-heeled black shoes. I wondered if they were too small. She shifted from foot to foot, adjusting her stance every few seconds. Next, she lifted one foot to rub it against her shin. I was enjoying her attempts to be professional while in pain.

"Cover-up what?" I asked again. Detective Millicent was developing some kind of theory about the case. The theory included me as some part of the crime.

She stuttered, "Well, i-i-i it was your e-e- e ex-husband who was k-k killed. Maybe you're protecting yourself." The last statement made Detective Millicent stand taller.

"How ridiculous," I said. "You're saying I trashed my expensive furniture, walls, and carpet to cover up––just what, exactly? "

. . . .

UNCLE JACK WALKED IN and saved her from what was going to be a major take-down.

"Good morning, Ms. Williams, Detective Carl. Looks like we have quite a mess here. Do we know what happened? I guess not or else we wouldn't have all the hullabaloo going on at headquarters right now." Uncle Jack walked around the apartment then ordered Millicent to the car for his camera.

"The crime scene photographers have already been here, sir."

Uncle Jack gave her the " just do it" look and said, "The camera is in the trunk. Here's the key."

As soon as Detective Millicent closed the door behind her, Uncle Jack turned to me, saying, "Lolly, what the fuck is going on here? They tell me the real murder weapon was found here."

"Yes, that's what they are saying. The knife was right over there on the credenza. It was some guy. He came up the steps, tried to get into my room, and laughed when I told him to go away. I came downstairs to find this mess——minus all the fingerprint dust."

"Well, now you're part of the mystery. You'll need separate representation. I've asked your Daddy to come over and take charge until we find out what's going on." He sighed and shook his head. "I can't believe you were talking to Millicent without representation. You know you can't trust yourself in these situations. People have a natural tendency to defend themselves and end up talking too much."

"I'd be worried if it was anyone but her. She wouldn't know a clue if it was break dancing in front of her eyes."

Detective Millicent Carl walked back in as if on cue. "Ms. Williams, the Captain wants to know if you can come down to the station."

· · · ·

IT WAS LATE AFTERNOON when Daddy arrived. He was sober, dressed in one of his tailored suits, shaved and manicured. He reminded me of the well-respected lawyer and judge I remembered from my childhood. The man who was once on a shortlist for the Supreme Court.

We were sitting on the stools around the kitchen island. Somehow, the kitchen was untouched by the paint. "There are cameras in front of the building with reporters yelling questions. They want to know why anyone would vandalize your apartment and if it had anything to do with Anthony's murder."

"I guess they don't know about the knife."

"Probably not for long. There is a major leak at the department." He walked toward the bar but stopped and looked at me as if to say, "I'm going to try to leave the booze alone."

He continued speaking. "I didn't invite Quentin or Nancy under the 'trust no one rule'. They were preparing to come here when I called. Let's wait until we have a strategy."

I felt my eyes widen. "Daddy, I'm the queen of strategy. This thing is moving too fast with too many surprises to devise a strategy. Right now, I just want to keep from falling off this roller coaster. This is a mess. I am so sorry I got involved."

I waited to hear his reaction. He had none. "There will be another surprise. If that knife was the murder weapon, my fingerprints will probably be on it."

"Lyla, please tell me you didn't touch it."

" Daddy, it *was* once my knife and I'm sure I touched it at least once. If for nothing other than putting it in the drawer."

Nancy, using her key, walked in with Quentin. "Sorry to disturb," Nancy said. "I thought you might want to hear this bit of news from us ASAP."

I was holding my breath when she said, "Carol has disappeared."

I must have looked like I would fall out of the chair. Quentin rushed to put his hands on my shoulders. Daddy's face registered a questioning expression as he watched Quentin's gesture. He wouldn't be the first to think there was something beyond work between us.

Nancy continued, "I tried calling her this morning to set up an appointment for hearing prep. I must have called at least 10 times, sent three texts, and even an email." She threw up her hands. "Nothing. Quentin went to the house."

He took up the story from there. "I knocked on the front and back doors before I decided to go to the basement." Quentin looked around to make sure we were listening, then said, "The door was unlocked. I went in."

"Why in the world would you do that?" Daddy asked.

"Well, she might be dead or injured."

"Oh my God," Daddy puffed. "Is this some charade of a TV crime show? Breaking in houses. Fingerprints all over the place."

"No sir, absolutely no one saw me," Quentin responded. "I always have crime scene protective gear with me. I was wearing gloves and a cap. I covered my shoes before I walked inside. There may be some footprints in the yard, but my sneakers are very ordinary and it hasn't rained in over a week.

"Not all of her clothes were gone but enough to notice empty spaces in the closet and on the shoe shelves. I checked the lingerie drawers, same thing. I checked the bathroom and found toiletries were missing as well as make-up."

We all sat without speaking to contemplate this new information.

Daddy broke the silence. "I'll have the captain postpone our meeting. I still have some pull down there."

I asked Nancy to call Uncle Jack.

• • • •

UNCLE JACK DIDN'T CALL right back or come over. We turned on the news to see a regular "shit storm" of information. The media had nearly everything. My checking account information, Carol's past employment, the trashing of my apartment, and the discovery of another possible murder weapon. What they didn't have? The connection to the mob family. At least not yet.

My picture occupied the background screen of every network. Only a single channel bothered to find a flattering one.

Nancy, Quentin, and I convened in my bedroom to watch the news on my television and all our laptop screens. Watching our careers disintegrate on national media was devastating. Especially knowing it would only get worse.

We ordered a pizza for dinner. The front desk called to say the delivery person couldn't get past the media and could I have someone come to the service entrance to pick it up?

Quentin went. The later editions of the news pictured him peeking from the door with the headline, "Famous lawyer holed up in an apartment as assistant grabs food delivery." The picture made even Quentin look ugly.

"At least go to a hotel," Daddy said. "I'll call and reserve a room in my name. I'll pick up the key, and give it to you. You just go to the room. If you don't go wandering around, they won't find you for a few days." I slipped out through the garage.

· · · ·

I WAS RESTING AT THE Ritz Carlton when my cell phone rang. "Hi. This is Carol."

I wasn't surprised. She was out on bail and didn't seem stupid enough to run. *But how did she get my private number?*

"Jean-Rene gave it to me."

"Where are you?"

"I'm with my mother at a friend's house. It's very nice. They have security. After the incident at your house, Mother got scared and came to get me. I can't go out of the area, so we decided to hang out here for a few days. Can you come? Mother thinks we need to talk."

Mother thinks? "Let me see if I can get Quentin to bring me there. What's the address?"

Quentin came for me in his personal car - a vintage blue Volkswagen Alfa Romero. I knew his parents owned a sleek Lincoln convertible they hardly drove. Plus, a pool car from the firm was available for general use.

The Volkswagen was tight, "Why did you bring this?" I asked.

"Well, I loaned the Lincoln to a friend and a pool car would be too easy for the press to identify. Hardly anyone knows about this car."

I shoehorned my way into the cute but tiny car and we took off, its four-speed, manual transmission quickly accelerating. He kept the car in good shape.

"I didn't know you were into cars."

"I'm not, really. Its my parents first car, so it's precious to them. I make sure to keep it serviced."

. . . .

DISCUSSING QUENTIN'S upbringing was uncomfortable for me. He was in foster care until he was eight. As cute as he was, it was difficult to find a family to adopt him. There was virtually no information on his family background, and most prospective families were cautious about his lack of history. He may have inherited some dangerous genes.

Finally adopted by an older couple who had been fostering him for a year or so. They were nice and gave the child as much as they could—not much.

Fortunately, he was genius-level smart and able to get scholarships to private schools and colleges.

So here he was, this successful striver, carrying around a notorious lawyer, hiding in a forty-year-old car.

I was just finishing the thought when the shot rang out. I am pretty sure they were aiming for me, but they hit Quentin.

He lost control of the car, and I instinctively grabbed the steering wheel. "Don't do that," he said, much more calmly than I would have expected.

The second shot hit me. Quentin steered the car to the shoulder of the road and call 911. In a move that seemed like a magic trick, a gun appeared in his hand. He pulled us both behind the tiny car and pointed the gun, poised to shoot. I could see Quentin was bleeding, but not from where; then, I must have passed out. I remember nothing until I woke up in the hospital.

. . . .

THERE WAS AN IV IN my arm and a swarm of people around me, yelling instructions and looking nervous. I could hear someone saying my blood pressure was dropping, and I needed to get to surgery in a hurry. I hurt all over. I couldn't tell where on my body I was shot.

Then I noticed Quentin. His bandaged arm caught my eye, but he was standing tall, looking ok. He was gripping my hand. "You'll be fine," he said as they pulled me away.

"I know," I replied.

• • • •

BUT I DIDN'T KNOW. When I woke up with monitors surrounding me, my arms full of needles, and bags of liquids over my head, I freaked, thinking I must be close to death. It didn't help that my father was sitting in a chair next to the bed, looking ten years older than I last saw him.

My first question is, "Where's Quentin?"

"He's ok," Daddy answered. "He got shot in his bicep. Nothing bad. He might not look so defined in his workout stuff for a while." Daddy chuckled. " He's in the hallway with Jack, Nancy, and a few other people. But first, do you know how or why this happened?"

"Carol called. We were on our way to meet her at a friend's house. We were driving on the highway when we were shot. I didn't even see the car. Like they say on TV, 'it all happened so fast.'"

"There are police here with questions. I'll get them to come back tomorrow. But Jack is going to want to talk to you. He convinced Millicent to go home by saying he'd question you. Fortunately, Quentin saw more than you, so at least we know the car's color. I'll let him come in first. He's the one who called me. He was pretty upset when I got here. By the way, he donated the blood for you. It's Monday, and they used their supply of your type on other shootings during the weekend."

Daddy was walking out the door when the nurse walked in. "You have a bunch of people out there. You can only see one at a time for five minutes each. I suggest no more than four more people total. I guess you'll want to see your son first."

I was about to say, "What son?" when I realized it was an honest mistake; she thought Quentin was my son.

"Please let him come in."

Quentin looked tired but otherwise ok. "I told them I was your son to check you in. I hope that's OK."

"It's OK. Thanks for the blood."

"Luckily, we're the same type. How are you feeling? They told me you took a bullet to your side. It nicked your pancreas and liver. You lost a lot of blood. You've apparently been taking blood thinners for a while.

"The doctor says you should be home in a few days."

Quentin was acting awkward, meek even. Not the glib, cavalier young man I usually spoke to. "Did this frighten you?" I asked.

"Yep. We've gotten in over our heads, I think."

"I believe they're after me. You were just driving."

"Maybe." He seemed to ponder.

"You need to get some rest," I said. "Ask Jack if you can stay with him. I can't imagine they would break in there. By the way, when did you start carrying?"

"I've been going to the gun range for a while. I have a holster under the seat of the car. I'm an ok shooter, but I'd have to practice more if I want to reliably shoot somebody."

"I was surprised to see the gun, but I'm glad you had it."

"By the way, Carol's mother invited me to stay with them. They say the house is guarded by a security service and is practically impenetrable."

I guess mob people are always surrounded by security.

I didn't respond. It sounded like a strange offer, and I couldn't understand why Quentin seemed to consider it.

"I'll see you tomorrow. Get some rest," he said.

I was sleeping again within seconds.

• • • •

THE WOMAN STANDING at the foot of my bed was as beautiful as advertised. I don't know how long I slept, and at first thought, she was part of my dream, but when she smiled, something familiar came through. "Hello, Gigi," I said to my former mother-in-law. Anthony shared her smile.

"It is so good to know you're recovering well, Lyla."

What do I say to this woman who occupied an integral part of my life for over a decade, yet, was somebody I didn't even know existed until a few days ago?

"I don't know how well I'm recovering." I said, "I've been drugged most of the time I've been here."

"I've spoken to the doctors. They say you will probably be well enough to be released tomorrow. However, you will still need to be cared for."

She spoke to the doctors. What about privacy laws, HIPPA? Who is this woman? Oh, I forgot, I'm "married to the mob."

As if reading my mind, Gigi said, "I told them I was your mother-in-law." She laughed a bit, a velvety, sexy sound. "It was once true, and as far as I know, you haven't replaced me." Another laugh escaped her perfectly lipsticked mouth.

My morphine-induced brain fog wouldn't allow me a smart retort. Besides, I became occupied with how well this woman, who must now be in her late sixties, still dazzled. Perfect skin, luscious hair, fit body while I lay in the bed looking like, well, someone badly wounded and pretty much asleep for two days. *She must wonder what her son saw in me.*

"I came to introduce myself and to invite you to recover at my residence." Her voice had the same lyrical cadence as Jean-Louis. "I am staying at the home of a friend. It's very large, secluded, and well-protected. I think it would be perfect with all this media coverage.

"Quentin is already there, as is Carol, and Jean-Rene. As you feel stronger, you can all work on the case."

I was so focused on Gigi that I didn't notice Uncle Jack standing in a shadowed corner. "I think it's an excellent idea. You need to be somewhere safe until we figure out who shot you and why." He came to stand next to Gigi, "Your father agrees."

They made a very attractive couple.

. . . .

NANCY CAME IN AFTER they left. "Well, this is new," she said. "I don't remember you being shot before. You've become the major focus of international media attention. If you think you were on the news a lot yesterday, this has escalated to near OJ level. You should see the cameras outside. Your dad has put security outside the door.

"Anthony's mother is in town, attracting a lot of attention. That cute little Jean-Rene has been handling the media since the mob family got involved. All the press seems to think your getting shot has something to do with the mob and the twenty-one million. I must say I agree."

"I agree, too." I shifted in the bed as the pain returned.

"Gigi has already been here. She came with Uncle Jack. Nancy, this stuff is getting weirder.

"She offered a place in her rental home to me during my recovery. She said it's well-protected. Guards, dogs, alarms, and walls, I expect."

"I hope that's not something you are giving even a minute of thought. These people are dangerous. You've been shot, girlfriend, and we don't know by whom or why."

"Uncle Jack thinks it's a good idea."

"As much as I admire Jack, staying with the mob family is about the stupidest thing I've heard. As soon as you're ready, we're gonna abscond to a hotel on a planet far, far away until you're well enough to begin conquering the world again."

"I think Quentin is already at Gigi's place." I grimaced as the pain became sharper.

"See the little button over there? Good stuff, morphine. Push it a couple of times and you'll start feeling really good. No pain, real fast. I'll check on you tomorrow."

She started walking out of the room and stopped. "You should know; Carol came to the hospital right after the shooting. Very upset. She was driving Quentin's Lincoln. She seemed panicked. Her concern was not for you.

"Sweet dreams, my friend."

• • • •

I MET QUENTIN NEARLY seven years ago. It was February 10.

Nancy ushered him in and introduced us. She took her normal seat on the sofa with her tape recorder. We thought he was a potential client.

"It's my birthday," he said with a wide smile. He still looked like a child, his face a little chubby, his hair in locs, and little dimples at the corners of his generous mouth. He wore a blue wool blazer, a blue shirt, and a yellow tie with khakis. I remember wondering how long he'd owned what was probably his only dress-up outfit. It would only take a few years for his looks to mature. His face thinned into sharp cheekbones. His dimples disappeared, too. He now sported a hundred-dollar haircut and a tailored suit.

"I know you are wondering why I mentioned my birthday," he said.

I nodded yes. He surprised me with his opening statement. It seemed so childish. "Please get to the point," I said. "I need to be somewhere."

I expected dejection on his boyish face. Instead, he smiled wider. "Ms. Williams, I'm hoping you can give me a birthday present." I was getting agitated as he continued, "You see, I'm a second-year student at Georgetown Law. I've maintained an A-plus average throughout my academic career, starting in kindergarten."

Ok, so you're smart.

"To get to the point, I'm looking for an internship. I don't need to be paid much. This is my hometown, and I'll be staying with my parents." He chuckled."Free room and board.

"Besides, they're older, and I'd like to be close to them as much as possible. I'm going to finish at Georgetown and come back here to live and work. Maybe get a sociology degree like you did."

"Hmmm. Why this firm? If what you say about your grades is true, you can probably intern at one of the large firms in town."

"Yes, ma'am, I know. But you've been working on interesting cases and gaining quite a good reputation." I was intrigued.

"Plus," he continued, "this was your father's firm, and his name carries a lot of weight." He looked serious."You handle criminal cases, and most of your clients are black. I think I can be of some societal help."

"I see. I wasn't looking for an intern, but let me give it some thought. We'll do some background checking, and I'll get back to you."

Quentin opened the expensive briefcase on his lap. *No doubt a present from someone with high hopes for him. The high quality didn't match the rest of his clothes.* He handed me three folders.

"The blue folder contains my transcripts from high school through the present, including various academic awards I've received. The yellow folder contains letters of recommendation from my professors, my pastor, and other community members. The red folder has a generic, completed job application and my credit report. I also wrote a brief biography, but there's not much to say about my life yet.

"Please investigate all the information. I assure you it's valid."

Nancy and I were blown away. Our mouths agape as he walked from the room,. "We better latch onto him as fast as we can," Nancy said. "I'll check this information and let you know."

Of course, it checked out. Quentin started as an intern at the end of his second year and soon became critical to our operation. He worked for us during both his winter and spring breaks. For his birthday, I gifted him with his first suit. He wore the suit to his graduation and on his first day as an Associate.

There were two other associates, but Quentin's skills were much stronger than theirs. They didn't seem to mind when he immediately became the "go-to" person in the office and the person I relied on the most. Next to Nancy, of course.

We knew little about Quentin's life outside of the office. He spent so much time working, we assumed, much like us, he didn't have a social life. Nancy and I came to love him in a professional sort of way. I'd never considered having a partner since my father left the firm, but I was prepared to offer him a partnership by the end of his third year. Nancy convinced me to wait until at least his fifth year.

I discussed it with him, and he seemed thrilled. So, I felt betrayed when he came into the office not long after our discussion and said, "I have something to tell you. You're probably going to want me to resign. I've been offered a position at another firm, and I think I need to take it."

He handed me a blank envelope and left the room without additional conversation.

I laid the envelope on my desk and stared at it on and off for hours. At the time, I was in the middle of my break-up with Anthony, and losing Quentin seemed to be more than I could handle right then. He was much more than an employee to me. I considered the young man to be a good friend.

I waited until the end of the day to open what seemed to be his resignation letter. My sixth sense warned me there was disappointment inside, but I panicked and became confused by what was there.

I was looking at an official document recording the live birth of a male child, Baby Smith. He weighed eight pounds, five ounces and was twenty-three inches long. His mother's name was Jackie Smith, aged 17, his race black, and his father unknown. The child was born on February 10th, 1989.

I called Nancy into the office. Her face looked pained. "Quentin told me he has another job offer. He plans to leave right away. I asked him if he wanted more money, but he said no. He just needs to know if you want him to stay. It doesn't make any sense to me. What's he done wrong? Committed a major crime or something?"

I practically threw her the piece of paper. It felt like it was burning my hand. Nancy's eyes widened as she read it. She grabbed her chest. "He's the baby," she said. "Is Quentin trying to say he's your son?"

. . . .

"HOW LONG HAVE YOU KNOWN?" I asked Quentin. He was sitting in my office, across from me, next to Nancy, the only other person in my world who knew the circumstances of his existence. Massive windows stretching along a wall of my office were situated to catch the sunset. Normally a relaxing part of my day but on this day, it felt like the beautiful yellow-orange sun was incinerating a major part of my life, uncovering secrets best kept hidden.

Nancy and I spent the night reliving his birth. The most painful experience of my life so far. We talked to him the next day after everyone else left.

"When I walked into your office for the first time, I kept saying it was my birthday, hoping you would remember." He turned to look at Nancy and said, "It didn't register with either of you."

"How did you find out?" I asked.

"Adoption records were made public shortly before I approached you. I was able to get my complete file. There didn't seem to be much there. I thought it was a dead-end until I saw Nancy was with you during the birth. Her full name and contact information were listed.

"I still didn't know for sure, but your bio says you were away studying in Arizona during a time coinciding with when you would have been pregnant with me. I was able to get a DNA sample after I began my internship. We matched. "

He stared at me expectantly. I couldn't say anything. Did he expect me to jump from my chair and hug him? Did he expect me to say, "I'm sorry I gave you away?" I wasn't.

"Don't worry," he continued. "After our first meeting, I knew you would hang up if I called and said, 'Hello, I'm your son.'" He looked away from me, turning toward the window. "I still wanted to know you, so I pursued the job. It was clear you'd put my birth way back in your memory, even so, I wanted to know you."

He avoided my gaze. "My parents wanted me to talk to you long before now, but I couldn't take being rejected when I was younger. I'm thirty now and much stronger.

"When I got the job offer, I decided this was a good time to tell you. If you were angry, I could leave with no questions asked."

"Look at me," I said. "Do you want to leave?"

"No. I enjoy it here, and believe it or not, I've come to love you both." His eyes pierced into mine. "However, it's clear you want to hide me. I can't be your son. I have to stay unknown."

"There's no sense in me lying to you. Acknowledging you as my son would destroy other people besides me. But I don't want you to leave. I don't know how I feel about being your mother. I'll have to work on it, but I want to have you around, and not just because you're talented."

Quentin said one last thing before leaving the room. " I've identified my father. I expect he doesn't know about me, and I'm not at all interested in getting to know him."

. . . .

DESPITE THE PREDICTIONS of my friends and the medical staff, it took me five days to be released from the hospital. There wasn't anything drastically wrong, but my blood pressure wouldn't stabilize. Things de-escalated on the news front, so Nancy sneaked me to an Airbnb in the countryside, far from where anyone would expect to find my city-loving self.

Daddy stepped in to get an extension on Carol's court date. I was grateful. I didn't have much time to prepare a case and was planning to ask for any charges to be dropped due to lack of evidence. Despite all the excitement and scandal around the case, there was nothing to prove Carol killed Anthony. The charges might have already dropped if not for all the drama. No doubt, DA Ashley Phillips probably hated the media attention she and her office were receiving. Negotiating dropped charges or at least minor charges would reduce attention and make her life easier. But she was a proud woman, unlikely to give up on a case she thought she could win.

So I wouldn't be followed, Nancy arranged for an Uber to take me to the rental house. As soon as the car door closed, my body sank into relaxation. By the time the car reached the place, a deep, drug-free sleep consumed me. The driver dropped my luggage inside the door, and I stumbled around the rambling single-story house until finding a bedroom. Fully clothed, I sank into another deep sleep. I woke up the next day, still feeling a dull pain but, to my surprise, refreshed.

Although I lived by myself, I was never alone. Street noises, televisions, ringing phones, and the hum of various electrical conveniences provided the soundtrack for my single life. In this mid-century modern house, I heard nothing but birds and breezes rustling the leaves on trees. Only the refrigerator hummed. I should have felt uncomfortable, not the almost limp sensation of calm. I was unwinding. I was alone.

Stumbling barefoot into the kitchen, I spotted a note perched beside the coffeemaker.

Push the red button and this machine will make coffee. You will find fresh fruit in the refrigerator and pre-made lunches and dinners from Luigi's. Just put them in the microwave when you're hungry. There are a few bottles of wine and a fifth of Jack Daniels on the counter. You're set for two weeks.

I have your phone. I have purchased two new ones for you; they are not traceable. Please, put one on your nightstand plugged in. Carry the other with you. Please try to keep it charged as you move around the house and outside. No one should call on either phone but me. You should only call out in an emergency, except for me.

The owners of the house have left a 12-year-old Toyota in the garage. It runs.

Around noon, a woman named Sarah will arrive. She will check on your health and all that involves. She will also warm your lunch, clean up, do laundry, and run errands. Sarah will be there until about five. She can warm and serve your dinner.

The TVs are ancient—local channels only. There is a radio. Remember radio? There's one in the bedroom and another in the kitchen. I recommend NPR. They've not been interested in the case. There are also tons of books.

Enjoy! Get some rest. Between your Daddy, Quentin, and me, everything should go smoothly with the office.

Love, your bestest friend.

Quentin opened his eyes. *Good. It's not daylight.* He sat up, swung his long legs to the floor, and looked over his shoulder to see what he dreaded. Carol asleep, naked, and in bed with him since the night before. As if he expected otherwise, he looked at his groin and found himself naked, too.

Damn, damn, damn, he cursed himself. He swiftly dressed in sweats and running shoes. As he slipped from the bedroom door, he asked himself, *What the fuck am I doing?* And determined he had no excuse for last night nor the many previous nights he found himself sleeping next to Carol.

Sneaking, he called it. Sneaking and about to get himself in deep doo doo. *You're smarter than this.* He imagined Lyla saying those same words when he confessed it all.

He needed to confess to someone who could help him. As soon as the affair was discovered, he would become the primary suspect in Anthony's murder. His biological mother would probably disown him, except she'd never owned him. *To her, I'm just a mistake of her past. A valuable mistake until now.*

Quentin started jogging around the grounds of Gigi's rented compound. He jogged past the main residence, a large castle-like building with several smaller buildings surrounding it. There wasn't a track but a gravel road connecting the house to the various outbuildings and the guardhouse by the entrance gate.

His thoughts focused on his situation with Carol. At first, he thought he might be in love, but later, she became a compulsion. A sorry, sorry involvement he couldn't stop.

Somebody on his side needed to know. Criminals surrounded him. He and Lyla were at risk of being killed. They'd been lucky; next time, they might be dead.

Maybe I should start by telling Jack. He's a man and might understand. No. He hardly acknowledges my presence unless he needs me for something.

Judge Williams? My grandfather? He's drunk most of the time and would probably shoot me for being so stupid. What's the quote about not suffering fools? It's probably his mantra.

His jog became an anxious run, causing him to sweat, increase his heart rate, and stress his muscles beyond his endurance. He fell. Sitting on the grass, recovering his strength, he watched the cloud-covered sunrise and talked to Nancy.

· · · ·

"WHAT!" NANCY YELLED. They were sitting in Lyla's office. When they looked at the empty chair behind her desk, an angry spirit surrounded them. "I suspected something when you told us you sneaked into her house. It sounded too easy. Like you'd done it before."

After his confession, Quentin's body sank into the chair, and he sat bent over with his head in his hands. "This is no time to be contrite," Nancy said. "You should have started feeling disgrace when she first seduced you." She shook her head for several seconds.

"She was an escort. I called a service to get a date for a fraternity event. They sent Carol. This was before she and Anthony were together but after Lyla's divorce. We became tight. More friends than anything else.

"Then she 'met' Anthony. Carol and I were at dinner. Anthony came by the table to say 'hello' to me. He was alone, so we asked him to join us.

"Before long, I wasn't hearing from her. Then she called to tell me she was no longer an escort, she was with Anthony. I don't remember if she said they were married.

"It wasn't even six months before she called me to say she was unhappy. Anthony was always comparing her to Lyla. To him, Carol just wasn't good enough. He married a whore. He was ashamed."

Nancy noticed Quentin sink lower into the chair. He was crying. "Get yourself together," Nancy said. "You're a grown man. There's no sympathy here. You certainly can't cry when you explain this to Lyla. And Jack. And Daddy Williams. You've been set up. We all have. They'll have to know.

"And eventually so will Millicent and the DA. So buck up, child. Now tell me the rest."

He slowly stood, walked over to the large windows, and picked up a decorative glass orb from a collection on the windowsill, tossing it from hand to hand.

"Well, at first, I was just trying to help her. Then the sex started. It got intense. We couldn't stay apart. Anthony started traveling a lot, so we started seeing more and more of each other.

"After a while, I began thinking about how risky it all was, began to feel uncomfortable, and wanted out. But I couldn't make myself stop. Then Tony was killed and I knew I needed to stop but, again, she needed me."

"Did you kill the man?"

Quentin shook his head. "No, and I don't think Carol did either. I was with Carol at their house the night Anthony was killed."

He hesitated to let the confession sink in. "Anthony spent most nights at work. We would meet at their house. I would park at the nearby grocery store, away from the cameras. She would pick me up. I would hide in rhe back seat until we got in the garage. My return would simply reverse those steps.

"You don't need to go through the kitchen to get to the garage, so I don't know if Anthony was dead when I left. But Carol was with me most of the night."

QUENTIN DIDN'T GO BACK to the compound. He couldn't bear looking at Carol and thinking what a fool he'd been. Because of his recklessness, he was the obvious person to be blamed for Anthony's killing. He would probably be at least questioned when news of the relationship became public.

"You've been thinking with the wrong head," Nancy said as their conversation ended. "It's time to start directing your brain toward wiggling your way out of this mess."

It was a short drive from the office to his parents' house. The house where he still lived. His mother's dementia was worsening. His father's response was a profound depression. Quentin was struggling with the idea he would soon lose both his parents—his only real family.

Eleanor and Fred James were in their late fifties when Quentin came to live with them. A retired banker and a schoolteacher, they decided their life's mission was to help black children growing up without the advantages given white kids. They already fostered several children and were beginning the process of quitting when Quentin landed on their doorstep full of distrust and hostility but smart beyond their understanding. An intelligence he kept to himself. Because Eleanor taught special needs children, she teased him out of his cocoon of anger. The couple came to love him, adopted him, and guided him to be the person so many people now respected. His parents were proud of their son's success and he would be forever grateful.

Quentin walked into a house smelling like dinner. His father was in the kitchen, pseudo-helping the housekeeper/nurse, Florence, prepare the meal. His mother had a rare moment of near lucidity when he walked in. "Quentin, you're home from school. How was football practice? Go wash up," she said from her wheelchair. "I cooked your favorite." She was smiling.

Dinner tasted bland. Since Eleanor stopped cooking, he usually found an excuse to eat out. He pushed the food around on his plate while watching Florence try to feed his mother. Looking agitated, she kept trying to push the caregiver's hand away. Food was accumulating on her face. Quentin went to help but, while he did better than the caregiver, he only managed a spoonful of the meatloaf. *She knows it tastes bad. I need to make different arrangements for meals.*

Fred was looking everywhere but at his wife. *This is bad for me, it must be unbearable for him.* Quentin was trying to engage him in conversation when the doorbell rang. "Probably Amazon," Florence said as she went to answer the door.

She came back with a face telegraphing something bad was happening. Two burly men and Millicent followed her.

"Quentin, I didn't want to do this in front of your parents but we haven't been able to find you since the shooting," Millicent said, sighing. "Quentin James, I'm here to arrest you as a suspect in the murder of Anthony Lewis, also known as Tony Louis. You are also being charged with money laundering. You have the right to remain silent."

One of the burly men grabbed Quentin to put on handcuffs. Eleanor started screaming, "That's my son, you can't take my son! Fred, stop them! STOP THEM!" Eleanor picked up her plate and threw it at Millicent, barely missing her.

"Don't cuff him." Millicent said to the officers, "Let's just go."

Quentin was escorted to the police car, trying to close his ears to the anguished sound of his mother screaming, "Stop them PLEASE stop them."

• • • •

HE EXPECTED TO BE TAKEN to the police headquarters, but he was at the neighborhood precinct sitting in an interrogation room, probably in use since the 1950s. The walls were institutional green and the doors and trim were putrid browns. Both looked painted over so many times the paint looked like it could separate from the surface.

He stared at the two-way mirror, looking like an imperial eye, judging his every move. As he inhaled the air made suffocating by decades of cigarette smoke, he wondered if Millicent was on the other side of the mirror hating him.

Millicent might become a problem. Her attraction to him was obvious from the beginning, and Lyla encouraged him to get close, pump her for information. He'd only gotten little tidbits, nothing important, but he led her to believe he was interested in something romantic. He'd taken her to dinner a few times. They discussed their common interest in movies, music, and political issues. At the end of the evening, he shook her hand, no kissing but, he could tell a kiss would have been ok with her.

During their time together, he realized she was not as dumb as they thought and after a while; she guessed his motives.

After what felt like an hour, but was probably twenty minutes, Millicent walked in with Jack Gerard. They sat across from him and began opening folders. "Just like on 'Law and Order,'" Quentin nervously tried to joke.

Jack said, "I hope you don't think this is funny, young man. You're in serious trouble."

It took some time for them to stop shuffling papers. Quentin was getting more nervous, knowing what he was about to hear. Jack spoke first. "Carol Lewis has confessed her part in the murder of Anthony Lewis. She says she witnessed you kill him in a jealous rage. Oh, and her only guilt was not telling sooner.

"She also says you are partly responsible for the $20M in Lyla Williams' bank account. The other part of being responsible belongs to her dead husband."

Quentin expected to hear about the affair, something that didn't make him a murderer. But Carol's written testimony made for a strong murder case without discussing the intimate relationship. "I need a lawyer. I have no comment," Quentin said, sitting straighter in the chair affecting his best *I'm above all this* demeanor.

"You sure do," Jack responded. "Millicent will help you make your phone call."

Millicent was silent as she led him to the booking desk to be photographed and fingerprinted. She was not speaking as they walked to an office for him to make his call. When he finished she, without a word, turned him over to a police officer to be escorted to his cell.

. . . .

THE CELL WAS CLEAN and well-used. Muted pine scent-tinged urine smells filled the air. Covered with graffiti,the walls made profane statements about the legal system, and prisoner names with dates. *Why would someone want to publicize their time in jail?*

Quentin was sitting on a neatly made bed with clean sheets and a nubby blanket when the police officer came to his cell. "Your lawyer is here."

He escorted him to the same room where Jack and Millicent brought him for questioning.

Waiting for him was one of the other firm's associates, John. Quentin was relieved; he couldn't imagine facing Lyla. "Hi. I'm here because no one can find Lyla. We'll keep looking but if we can't find her. Judge Williams will be handling your arraignment. I'm sure you know at this late hour, your arraignment won't happen until tomorrow. How are they treating you?"

"I'm in jail, but it's cleaner than I expected. I'm the only person back there. That'll probably change as it gets later."

"Is there anything you want me to tell Judge Williams?"

"You can tell him I'm not guilty."

. . . .

QUENTIN SAT AT THE plaintiff's table in the county courthouse with The Judge sitting next to him. His hands and legs shackled, he looked straight ahead and tried to detach himself from the proceedings. He envisioned his image was being projected on television screens throughout the country and tried not to cry. Pain and embarrassment blurred his vision, but the sound of the proceedings came through clearly.

"Judge Kennedy," the bailiff said, "Quentin David James is next."

"What are the charges?"

Ashley spoke next. "Mr. James is charged with first-degree murder and two counts of money laundering." Her voice sounded like someone gloating.

"Well, this is surely the most interesting case of the morning. Is Mr. James represented by counsel?"

"Yes, sir. Franklin J. Williams, Esquire." The booming, erudite voice of The Judge resonated through the speaker. "Partner emeritus of Williams and Williams Attorneys at Law."

"It's been a long time since I've seen you in court, Judge Williams." There was a smile in Judge Kennedy's voice. "Is your client ready to plead?"

"Your honor, Mr. James pleads not guilty to all charges." The Judge's voice was confident.

With the Honorable Judge Williams as his counsel, Quentin wondered how anyone could doubt his innocence.

Judge Williams continued, "Except for his college years, Mr. James has been a local resident. He's not previously been charged with any crime. He has only one traffic ticket. Mr. James holds a responsible job, is respected in his profession, and when not working, takes care of his elderly parents, who are both in ill health. They would probably need to move to a care facility if Mr. James is not available. Therefore, I ask that bail be remanded in this case.

"His father is in the courtroom. Mr. Fred James, please stand."

Quentin fumed as he imagined the small, sad person who was his adopted father, standing as an exhibit for the court.

He didn't have long to think about it before Ashley's angry voice spoke up, "Your honor, these are capital crimes, involving drug traffickers with worldwide contacts. We have credible statements from witnesses to verify Mr. James' involvement with criminals."

"Your Honor, I can assure you those statements are false and will be thrown out at the preliminary hearing. Your witnesses are culpable themselves." The Judge said in an even tone, countering Ashley's angry voice.

"Nevertheless," the judge said, "these are very serious charges. I'm setting bail at one million dollars."

· · · ·

QUENTIN WALKED INTO the courthouse lobby with a plastic bag carrying his personal belongings. Judge Williams, Nancy, and his adoptive father were waiting.

"Your father put up the bail," The Judge said.

"They're holding the house and the cabin as collateral," Fred added.

"Dad, I'll give you the money so you can get the title back."

"If they haven't already," The Judge said, "the Feds will put a hold on all your assets. You're lucky they didn't ask for a cash bond."

"I was raised by old people. I have a stash."

"Well, don't broadcast it. They'll come for the stash, too. By the way, how did you accumulate enough money to have that much money in cash?"

"I've called Lyla. She'll be here this evening." Nancy interrupted. "Go home with your Dad. I understand your mother's upset."

I decided there was a lot recommending this relaxation stuff. Sarah came every day to dress my wound. She warmed my gourmet lunch and dinner, served me, and poured my wine. I'd never experienced this kind of quiet and comfort. It was wonderful. Three whole days of wonderfulness.

I was taking a twilight walk around the property, thinking about the spa tub, when the phone in my pocket rang. It was Nancy bluntly stating, "Quentin's been arrested. They've charged him with Anthony's murder and money laundering."

I know Nancy heard me gasp, but she wasn't giving me any time to ask questions, not yet anyway. "It seems he's been knocking knees with Carol for quite some time.

"She and her mother have signed an affidavit accusing him of murdering Anthony and participating in a money-laundering scheme including the money parked in your newly found bank account."

I was breathless as I ran back to the house. I needed to pack. Nancy continued, "Carol was a witness to the murder, so she says. A jealous rage. She admits to helping Quentin cover it up. I haven't seen the statement. I just have what Jack told me.

"Supposedly the statement says Quentin helped Carol set up bank accounts to facilitate the transfer of funds to shell companies, so-called start-ups."

"How long have Quentin and Carol been together?"

"Since right after your divorce."

I was back in the house, sitting on the bed to catch my breath. "What does Gigi have to do with this?"

"She convinced Carol to confess all the sordid details. The Jean-Rene guy is handling everything from their side."

"Where is Quentin now?"

"He was arrested yesterday, kept overnight, and arraigned this morning. One million dollars bail. Your Dad handled the arraignment. Quentin's father put up their property as collateral. He's at his parent's house now.

"Millicent participated in the arrest with two precinct cops. Ashley is the DA on the case."

"Are you coming to get me or should I drive the Toyota?"

"I'm on my way now but we have time to get our arms around this before the preliminary hearing. Get some more rest."

"You think resting is going to happen, now?"

• • • •

I WAS BENT OVER, MY head in my hands. A position I'd seen my desperate mother take many times during my youth. I was thinking, *How do I fix this? When* I felt something cold against my temple and turned to see Uncle Jack standing with the business end of a gun against my head.

He wasn't smiling. His expression said he wanted to kill me. I waited a few seconds for him to speak, but he just glared with eyes looking as if they could send lightning bolts across the room. I gulped and said, "If this is supposed to be a joke, it doesn't look like either of us is laughing."

"No joke. I am angry enough to kill you but I really should have done it years ago." He walked across the room and sat on a dressing chair in front of a vanity.

"You didn't know about this years ago," I said.

"No, and the fact I didn't know didn't make it any less dangerous. You fooled me, Lolly. You were playing games with my life. Games that could have put me in prison for a long, long time.

I wish I could have felt some remorse, but I just wanted out of this conversation and my Uncle Jack out of my sight.

"What did you do with the money I gave you?" He didn't stop glaring.

Jack has never been violent, but maybe now is the time he breaks character. "I bought a plane ticket to Arizona. I took a couple of courses until it was time for him to be born, then I came back here."

"So stupid. So stupid. But I dropped you off at the clinic."

"And I didn't go in. There were tons of people yelling with signs and gross pictures of fetuses. They scared me. I left, met up with Nancy, got ice cream, and hatched a different plan.

"Damn it! I was barely seventeen. At first, I was having silly romantic notions about staying in Arizona, raising the baby myself. After a while, I became disgusted with what was happening to my body. I couldn't wait to give him to somebody else and reclaim my life."

"Why did you come back here? Why didn't you leave him in Arizona?"

"I'd made arrangements with a home for unwed mothers before I left. I didn't want to be alone when the baby was born, so I sneaked back home and into the facility when my time was near. Nancy stayed with me during his birth. I was scared. At that point in my life, I'd hardly broken a fingernail. The thought of giving birth was a bit much for me."

I walked to the living room and poured both of us a drink. Uncle Jack followed me.

"Plus, I think my childish self had visions of you saving me and the baby and I wanted to be here just in case. Fortunately, you didn't and he turned out well. Way better than either of us would have done."

"Quentin seems to have inherited your brain, but I don't think he got your callousness," Jack said as he downed the drink in one gulp.

"You didn't care that this could have sent me to jail? Even now, I'll probably lose your father as a friend, not to mention the respect of the rest of my world."

"I'll tell the truth, Jack. It wasn't at all your fault. You were drinking, went to bed, I took advantage, and you woke up with me. It was just supposed to be a prank."

"Well, I guess I'm still being pranked. I've been pulled from the case for being too close to the family. Ashley made the call. I don't know if she knows how close."

"Quentin knows you're his father. He researched and took a DNA test to find us. He's known since law school and identified both of us before he walked into my office for the first time."

"He knows? The few times I met him, he hardly spoke to me!"

"He told me he doesn't want to know you. I'm not sure why."

"He probably thinks I'm a pedophile who raped his innocent child mother."

"I was never really a child and certainly not innocent. Just a dumb kid."

· · · ·

NANCY ARRIVED AND JOINED us at the whiskey bottle. "His parents are traumatized. His mother has dementia but was alert enough to see the police take him away. She needed to be sedated. A horrible thing for a woman already losing her mind."

The tension in the room was dense. Nancy said, "I know we're all worried about Quentin but what else is going on here?"

"He knows **all** about Quentin," I said, looking at Uncle Jack.

Nancy said, "Yeah, I was pretty shocked, too. I thought he was smarter than to get involved with Carol. I didn't even know they knew each other before the murder."

"I didn't either. But, Nancy, Uncle Jack knows about Quentin's real parents."

"Oh." looking at Jack, she quipped, "How did you find out?"

"It wasn't hard after I thought about it. He made an off-hand comment in the interrogation room and laughed. I was caught off-guard. It was like my not-very-bright younger brother had come back to life. Scared me. His voice. His expression. Those eyes.

"I checked his files, found out he was adopted and when he was born, then I counted."

. . . .

WE SAT IN SILENCE UNTIL Nancy turned on the television. The heavy makeup of the "News team you can trust" team, Chad and Judy, shined as they walked us through the county fair, a fishing contest, the weather, and a cat video before getting to the news of the day.

"Today marked another amazing development in the evolving investigation into the murder of Anthony Lewis. Judy, what do we know?" Chad said cheerfully.

"Chad, let's take our viewers to the County Courthouse where our investigative reporter, Lovenia Jones is waiting to bring us up to date."

The screen switched to a young, nervous-looking woman standing by the courthouse sign. DA Ashley stood next to her. "I'm here with the County Assistant District Attorney on this case," she put the microphone in Ashley's face, almost hitting her nose, "I understand there's been a new arrest in the case. What can you tell us?"

"Not much, Lovenia. Last evening we arrested Quentin James, an attorney in the office of the Williams and Williams law firm as a suspect in the murder of Anthony Lewis. He was arraigned this morning on charges of murder and money laundering."

"Oh my," the investigative reporter feigned surprise, "wasn't he one of the attorneys for Carol Lewis, the murder victim's wife?"

"Yes, he was," Ashley answered, looking sternly through her near-inch-long black eyelashes and blue eyeshadow. 'Is she still a suspect?"

"Yes, she is."

"This is a very confusing case. Lots of twists and turns."

"Yes," Ashley replied. "That's all the information I can provide right now."

"Judy and Chad, back to you."

"Wow," Judy said.

Chad responded, "Wow is right. Tomorrow, the network is broadcasting a special report to help us work out some of the information in this tangled case."

"We need to find out what they have," Uncle Jack said as he walked from the house.

"I need to talk to Quentin," I said to Nancy.

"I'll come with?"

"No. I need to be alone on this one."

• • • •

I MET QUENTIN AT HIS parent's bungalow. The block was lined with houses of the same elevation. A unique paint color and landscaping to distinguish one from the other. There was a one-car garage, so I parked on the street. I envisioned the son I discarded growing up in this pleasant blue house with Adirondack chairs and a pot of geraniums on either side of the front door. It seemed quite 1950s Americana.

Dumbfounded is how I felt when an old white man opened the door. No one bothered to let me know white people adopted Quentin. I knew they were white, but this man looked like he could have been the great-grandfather. *It shouldn't matter. I gave him away, asking no questions, obviously not caring who got him.*

The small man greeted me by name and told me, "Quentin is in the kitchen, helping his mother. You're welcome to have a seat in the living room or you can follow me to the kitchen. Please remove your shoes. There are some slippers in the corner if you want them." I did as he asked, but without slippers.

It was a packed house, small rooms with too much furniture. I moved carefully to avoid bumping into something. Looking at the low ceilings, I imagined how claustrophobic the house must have felt as Quentin grew to over six feet.

The woman in the too-warm kitchen looked startled to see me. I could immediately tell there was something "not right" with her. "Who's the woman, Quentin?" she asked.

"I told you she might come by, Mama," he said, patting her hand. "This is my boss, Ms. Williams." The house was hot, and the heat was making me uncomfortable.

The woman's eyes narrowed. "Are you here to take him away from us?"

Quentin jumped in, "No, Mama. She doesn't want me. Don't worry. I'm yours forever." He smiled, kissed her on the cheek, rubbed her back, and his mother relaxed. *Heartbreaking.* I wondered if she'd spent years thinking I would try to get him back.

"Lyla, we need to talk. Privately. Mom, Dad, Ms. Williams, and I are going to talk in my bedroom."

Quentin slept in a small attic room decorated like he was still in high school. His spread was blue and covered with stars. Posters of famous sports figures hung on the walls. Shelves with trophies and certificates hung above a desk with textbooks stacked on it. The only thing showing the passage of time was his latest model Apple laptop.

"My mother likes to come up here. Since she's been getting sicker, it seems to make her more comfortable to have everything like it was years ago," he explained. "I don't know how much longer we can keep her at home, especially if I go to jail. It will kill Daddy."

Quentin had been avoiding my eyes, but now he turned to me, looking directly at my face. "I know Nancy has told you about Carol and me. I've known it was stupid for a long while, but I thought I was in love and needed to protect her. Deep down, as soon as it started, I knew it was a mistake."

He walked across the room to the tiny attic window and stood with his back to me. "My relationship with Carol is not the worst thing I have to talk to you about. Lyla, I have a sealed juvenile record."

I was sitting in his desk chair, watching him as he walked the few steps to sit on his bed. Wrapping my arms around my chest, I braced for what was coming next.

"When I was nine, I stabbed a boy at summer camp. We were fighting. He brought the knife, it ended up in my hand, and I stabbed him. It was an accident, but he was stabbed nonetheless."

My countenance seldom shows what I'm thinking or feeling, but a faint seemed to overtake me. Quentin saw what was happening and rushed to help me on the bed.

I came to with a towel on my head and Quentin trying to give me water. I pushed the glass aside. "Get me some bourbon."

"'Later, Lyla," he said. "You need to understand what happened.

"I hadn't been with my parents long, and they didn't understand it might be difficult for me to be in a camp with all white kids. The girls were alright, but the boys thought it was fun to harass me and push me around every day. There's always one who wants to show he's more alpha than the rest. One day, he charged me with a knife. He thought it was funny. I didn't and fought back. He dropped the knife; I grabbed it and stabbed him."

"Did he die?"

"No. I stabbed him in the arm. He didn't even bleed a lot, but they put me in juvenile detention and charged me with attempted murder.

"His parents pitched a bitch. A black kid with a knife stabbed their son but some kids took my side, and my parents got a good lawyer."

"Well, your sealed juvenile file is not admissible as evidence."

"I know. But, Millicent slipped me a note as I was leaving court. Ashley has the file. It won't be sealed for much longer."

Quentin watched Lyla as she recovered from the shock of his revelation. *It's strange. No words to ask me how I felt or if I got hurt in the fight. I don't even think she cares about the case anymore. Would she pay attention if I wasn't associated with her firm? Would she care about me getting convicted? No. I'm sure. She'll work like hell to clear me and it will become another of her miracles. Hooray, Lyla. Fuck the rest of the world.*

She calls Jack her uncle. Her pal. But he's her rapist. Shouldn't she hate him? I guess not. What did she say? "Knowing about you would hurt a lot of people. Destroy their lives." Mine included?

But I love her, don't I? For sure, I admire her. She needed to be strong, to be successful. She's masked her feelings for so long it's become who she is. Lyla wouldn't be successful if she were soft, malleable. Maybe she's not maternal or caring, but she has nurtured my career beyond what I could ever expect. Even before she knew who I was.

When they returned to the kitchen, Eleanor was sitting in her wheelchair, head nodding with sleep, but Fred was watching the stairwell, waiting for them to return.

"Quentin, take your mother to her room and get her into bed. I want to speak to you and Ms. Williams without upsetting your poor mother any more than she already is."

The kitchen was quiet as Quentin carried Eleanor to her room, laid her onto the double bed, and pulled the blanket and chenille spread up to her chin. When he returned, Lyla was sitting in his mother's space.

"What do you want, Dad?" Quentin asked.

"I want to know what's going to happen with my son. From what I understand, Quentin, you are accused of murder with a lot of evidence making you look guilty. Ms. Williams is representing one of your accusers. Where does that leave you?"

Lyla spoke up, "I am no longer representing Carol. At least I won't be in a couple of hours. I will be handling Quentin's defense."

As Quentin smiled, Fred said, "I hope you're not offended, Ms. Williams, but I think you should leave yourself out of Quentin's affairs."

Lyla looked startled as Fred continued. "I may not be a lawyer or as smart as you and my son, but, average as I may be, I can see some things clearly." he turned away from Quentin, focusing his attention on Lyla.

"My son is in a lot of trouble, Ms. Williams. All this trouble is about you. Your husband, your mother-in-law, and your sister-in-law. He needs a lawyer who is concerned about his innocence. That's not you."

Lyla looked ready to retort when Fred said, "I don't need any speeches or pushback from you, Ms. Williams. You may have given birth to my son, but you have never cared for him. You've only used him.

"You see, Eleanor and I have known you were his birth mother since he was nine. After his problem at camp, we thought we should know more about his background. I know that sounds racist, but it's where we were then. He could have been a crack baby or had a genetic problem we needed to treat.

We hired a private detective and looked for the worst. Instead, we found an upstanding well-to-do family.

"Seeking legal representation for Quentin, we sent a note to your father letting him know a very close relative needed help. We never heard back. Not a word. He was not interested to see if there was any truth to our note. We realized our son had no one but us.

"We advised Quentin against coming to work for you, but he fought us. Said he wanted to know you. We watched as you led him into your world and, even after knowing you were his birth mother, showed him little but superficial affection.

"Now, because of you, he may go to prison. He may lose everything he has worked so hard for.

"I can't be sure you're not the one framing him. I refuse to have you anywhere near my child, whether as his lawyer or in any other role. Get out of my house, away from my family, and our lives. Go away. I'll handle it from here."

Lyla stood with a huff and walked toward the door, with Quentin following her. He was apologizing to his father when a small voice came from the bedroom. "Quentin, please come. I need you." It was his mother.

I walked to my car barefoot, too upset to notice. I threw my shoes in the car and drove off so fast my tires squealed.

I hated these people. Hate is a word I seldom use, but something about Quentin's adopted parents caused my body to ache and encouraged me to hit someone. *Maybe it's just the father. His mother has dementia and has no idea about what's going on. Was she always whiny? Whatever, they're sad, pitiful people. It's a wonder Quentin turned out alright. Must have been his good genes.*

· · · ·

I WAS UPSET AND DIDN'T know what to do next, so I called Nancy. We met at our regular bar.

"If Quentin is being set up, somebody is doing a good job." Nancy was drinking shots. She gulped her second while talking, she had been drinking more than usual the last few days.

"But why, Nancy? Because of the relationship with Carol?"

I shook my head and said, "Someone feels threatened. There's more going on. I'm sure it's connected to them being together."

" For sure. He was in the house with Carol the night of the murder. He's not sure he was there when it happened.

He' s stupid, but not stupid enough to kill the husband of the wpman he's sleepin with." Nancy continued. "He wants tp break from her. I think she's trying to set him up. Especially if she did it."

"Kinda makes sense. But something seems off about your theory. Maybe he did it. Quentin has a temper. He stabbed a little boy when he was nine." Lyla explained the circumstances.

"He's been trying to look out for you. Think about it, Lyla. Quentin was genuinely surprised when Carol showed up asking for your help. He tried to dissuade you from the case. He knew there was going to be trouble beyond just defending her. Perhaps Quentin knew about the drug cartel connection."

Nancy asked the bartender for another shot and said, "You need to talk to Carol and her mother."

· · · ·

"I'M HERE SOLELY TO protect my daughter." Gigi was leaning back in a printed chintz slipper chair; I sat across from her in a solid green velvet wingback. Gigi looked relaxed and comfortable in the small sitting room of their rented house. *Me, not so much.*

Carol stared but didn't speak to me. Her mother said she was taking sedatives to deal with the trauma of everything. I laughed.

"What does protecting your daughter have to do with accusing Quentin?"

"Don't be silly, Lyla. He is a murderer. Carol was protecting Quentin out of love. She has now come to realize family love is more important than the sexual kind." Gigi shifted in her chair. "A truth every woman must come to realize at some point. It took the trauma of her brother's death to bring her to her senses."

I was astounded. *Did Gigi believe her bullshit? I was seldom wrong when reading a person, but with this woman, I couldn't tell.* "Why do you think that, Gigi? What leads you to think Quentin killed Anthony?"

"Because it's the only thing that makes sense. Carol was trying to get out of the relationship with Quentin for some time. Tony asked Quentin to leave her alone. Quentin objected. Tony came home on the night of his murder, found Quentin there, and ordered him to leave. Quentin picked up a knife and killed him." Gigi looked much older. "Knives seem to be his weapon of choice.

"I know you're very fond of Quentin, Lyla, but you must accept the facts as the evidence leads. He murdered my Tony. My only son." She cried.

A nicer woman might have found her a tissue. I'm not a nice woman. Her make-up smeared on her face and she was sniffling when I said, "This is a crock of shit. I don't believe it and neither should the DA."

Quentin expected to be rearrested as soon as the money laundering became known. He was in his office trying to bring his outstanding cases up to date when Jack walked in. He sat in one of the desk chairs without being invited. "How can I help you?" he asked.

Quentin wanted to laugh. Instead, he said, "Help me with what? Help me dig deeper into this hole I find myself in. No, sir. I think I'm in enough trouble. I don't need your help."

"Yes, you do, son. In fact, I'm the only one who can help you, I am the only one who knows you're innocent."

"I'm not your son. Please don't address me that way. I am the son of a smallish white man who just put his financial future on the line to keep me out of jail."

Ignoring Quentin's protests, Jack continued to talk. "For somebody so smart, you sure are stupid." he said, shaking his head. "You need to accept the realities of your life. Number One. I am your father. Two. Lyla is your mother, and all the trouble attached to being a member of that family is your baggage. My family is just a group of poor people trying to have a place to live and food to eat on a regular. If you end up going to jail, you'll probably have several of your cousins as neighbors.

"Three. Carol has been setting you up since before she met you. Anthony was part of it. And now, Gigi is following through.

"Four, you are going to need to own up to your involvement in Carol and Anthony's crimes to avoid a long jail sentence."

Quentin hated the man. Although he knew Jack could help him, he wanted the man out of his sight.

"I may share some of your DNA, Jack, but I don't want anything to do with a pedophile. You raped my mother, you piece of shit. How many other children have you raped?"

Jack kept talking as if Quentin hadn't uttered a word. "You're right. My reputation is about to go south. Your grandfather may try to kill me, but you need to get under the Williams family's stellar reputation to give you some cover. His name still carries a lot of weight in this community, and you might as well take advantage of it. He hasn't given you much else.

"I'm going to talk to him as soon as I leave."

"What don't you understand? I don't want anything to do with you. I don't want your help. I don't want Judge he Williams' help. I don't want either of you around. The only thing I want is to shed any association I have with you."

Jack left without another word.

· · · ·

QUENTIN WORKED WELL into the night and took a room at a cheap hotel, thinking no one would look there. He was wrong. The banging on his door started at five in the morning. He pulled back the plastic-lined curtain to see Jack and The Judge standing outside the door with coffee. He slid the gun, now a regular part of his apparel, under the bedcovers before answering the door.

"You can't hide as long as you have a cell phone," Jack said. "Did you forget? I got you a burner. We'll take the other phone to your office and leave it there."

"I was tired and not thinking when I left the office."

"You aren't much of a thinker, are you?" The Judge entered the conversation, sober again. Maybe it was getting to be a habit.

"You set up the false sale of the hotel," he declared. "What else did you do?"

The Judge was sitting on the bed; Jack in the desk chair. Quentin stood against the door, trying to decide how much to tell them. *Might as well tell them everything. It's going to come out, anyway.*

"I facilitated an investment in two tech start-ups in Virginia and another in California. I handled the purchase of a bar and a bowling alley here in town."

"Who did you think you were working for?"

"Anthony and Carol. They were being threatened by one of Carol's former clients. They would be killed if they didn't launder several million dollars. I took care of it all.

"I set up a company called C&A Investments which we sold to another company called Roundup, Inc. I don't know who they are."

"What about the money in Lyla's bank account?"

"It comes from the hotel sale. I didn't do that one alone. One of the blackmailer's representatives helped with the hotel. We provided them a place to hide the money until it could be laundered."

"The place was Lyla's bank account. Was there anything else involving my daughter?"

"No. Nothing I know about. Anthony suggested the bank account. I didn't know it was Lyla's."

It was Jack's turn to talk. "Carol and Gigi are set to talk to Ashley later this morning." He turned to The Judge, seeming to request approval before saying to Quentin, "I think you should turn yourself in before they get there and confess all this to Millicent and her new partner on this case."

The Judge added, "For the moment, I'm your lawyer."

Quentin didn't want him as a lawyer and said so.

The Judge's response, "I don't give a damn what you want. Soon, word of our relationship will be public, and I need to make sure you are in the best position possible to make a deal with minimal shame for my family.

"Grab your gun from under the covers, and let's get going. You slept in your clothes. Do you have a change at the office?"

. . . .

THE JUDGE PROVIDED prep information for the interrogation with Millicent and her new partner. "Ashley may join us so be very careful about what you say. She listens better than anyone I've encountered and picks up on the smallest inconsistency. I'll do most of the talking initially, and I'll cue you when it's time to speak. Don't volunteer anything."

"Have you forgotten I'm a criminal lawyer, Judge Williams?"

Jack didn't speak. The Judge directed him to get Quentin a change of clothes from the office and to leave the phone where it could be easily found.

Quentin kept two changes of clothes in the office: one business and the other casual. Jack brought the casual outfit—khakis, a tee-shirt, a jacket, and sneakers. The defendant looked more like a student than a money laundering suspected murderer on his way to confess.

• • • •

THE JUDGE DROVE THEM to the police station in his black Range Rover. The small group of media people waiting in front of the building was a surprise.

"How did the word get out?" Th Judge asked.

"I provided some of the early leaks in the case, but the more recent ones have come from someone else. Maybe someone with enough money to bribe a law enforcement official," Jack admitted. "I apologize. I thought maybe the publicity would scare Lyla off the case. When I saw she was enjoying the show, I stopped."

"Why would you want to scare her off?" Quentin asked.

"Because I knew there were dangerous people involved."

"That's why Jack asked me to come up from Florida," The Judge added. "She wasn't listening to me either."

He parked in a place reserved for court officials. He still had privileges. The space was across the street from the courthouse. There was a short walk before reaching the media. Quentin was trying to decide whether to hide his face or walk proudly when it happened.

It took seconds. There was a loud pop. Jack knocked Quentin to the ground and fell on top of his son. Another loud pop. Silence, then frightened animal-like, screaming and screeching accompanied by the steps of people running.

Jack's body was like a rock, keeping Quentin from moving. He tried to move his arm and found it covered in blood. Warm liquid covered his head, flowing toward his eyes. "Are you alright?" he yelled to Jack, but the pressure on his chest stifled his voice. He tried to move from under him. Jack was too heavy.

A crowd of faces appeared above him, positioning themselves for a good view. The Judge trailed a few steps behind.

Th Judge was on his knees, trying to check Jack's pulse. He put his head gently on his friend's body and, in a hoarse whisper, asked Quentin if he'd been hit. The large amount of blood made It was impossible to tell.

Ashley's loud voice was bellowing orders to the crowd, forcing them to move away. Millicent knelt beside The Judge to say an ambulance was coming. They knew the paramedics didn't have the magic needed to bring Jack back to life.

. . . .

QUENTIN WAS UNINJURED and wanted his parents to know. He called as the news was hitting the airwaves. Shocked and worried, they wanted him home. He shuddered at the thought of sitting in the cramped house.

Because the Judge vouched for him, Quentin was released from the hospital without being arrested. Instead of taking him to his parents, the Judge checked Quentin into a hotel under an assumed name, stating he was reasonably sure no one would find him there.

The cell phone that allowed Quentin to be tracked was still in Jack's pocket.

Thankfully, Jack and Quentin were the same size, so The Judge brought clean clothes from Jack's apartment before they left the hospital. As he changed from the clothes drenched with Jack's blood,

Quentin realized Jack took two bullets for him, saving his life. Quentin credited Jack's actions to law enforcement instincts, not fatherly love or concern.

Now at the hotel, exhausted and mentally fogged, Quentin went to sleep immediately,

* * * *

HOURS PASSED. THE SUN was high in the sky the next day when Quentin finally returned to life. The television came on, seemingly without help, as he woke. Still dazed, the newscaster's voice shocked him into alertness.

"We have more information on yesterday's courthouse shooting. Sargent Jack Gerard, a forty-year veteran of the police force, was killed by a sniper's bullet while trying to protect his son, Quentin James, accused murderer, embezzler, and money launderer. According to his grandfather, the former Judge Frank Williams, Mr. Gerard, and Mr. James were about to enter the courthouse when the shooting began. They planned to provide new information on the case.

"Neither Mr. James nor his mother, prominent attorney Lyla Williams, were available to provide statements. Ms. Williams is said to be in deep mourning, and Mr. James' whereabouts are unknown.

"We'll have more on this story tonight in a special 9 p.m. newscast."

While the newscaster spoke, a video of the shooting played on a steady rotation.

Scanning through the channels, he saw the same video on every news station, including the BBC and Telemundo, where the newscaster described the scene in Spanish. The BBC showed close-ups of Jack's dead, bloody body covering Quentin. Jack looked to be protecting his son. A picture of Quentin from the firm's website hung in the screen's corner, along with a picture of Jack in his police uniform. Quentin recognized a familial resemblance and went back to sleep.

I watched the news channels in a depressed stupor. After hearing from my sister, brother, and both nieces. I turned off the ringer and threw the phone in the dirty clothes hamper. I wasn't answering questions and just told them I was fine and much of what they heard was true.

"What much?" my oldest niece asked. "The much where you're a mother and Uncle Jack is the Dad? The much where that handsome young man in your office is my cousin and some sort of gangster, or the much where Uncle Jack was killed trying to protect the criminal?" I gave up on the phone. I'd always felt this niece was the most like me, and now I know it for sure.

I needed some advice. Some Uncle Jack advice, but he was dead. I called Nancy. Her advice was to drink whiskey. Already drunk, she came to help me.

We sat on my floor eating leftover Indian food when she said, "We need to get in touch with The Judge and Quentin. We need to talk strategy."

"Really? How am I supposed to face The Judge? Let's think about it. His best friend is dead, and by the way, his best friend got his innocent daughter pregnant at 16. He has a grandson who was kept hidden from him for over 30 years. The grandson is a criminal who, by the way, is responsible for his best friend's death."

"Yep. Those are the facts, but they don't change the fact shit is dropping all over us, and darling Quentin is on his way to jail."

"You can call them."

"I will."

· · · ·

THE JUDGE SUGGESTED they meet Quentin at his hotel. We arrived one at a time, looking as unidentifiable as possible, and took the elevator to the limited access floor, room 2031.

I arrived first and knocked on the door. No answer. I tried not to panic and walked to the lounge to grab several of those little bottles of Jack Daniels from the honor bar, just in case. Nancy walked in behind me and congratulated me on my wise choice. Then The Judge came. Refusing to look at me, he told us to get out of the lounge. *We might be identified.*

We gathered at Quentin's door while The Judge knocked and called. Still no answer. I was truly panicked. I could only think of the gun Quentin carried and how much he would be upset by the media coverage.

Nancy read my thoughts. "Black people don't kill themselves," she said.

"Another one of those lies we tell ourselves," Daddy said. "Stop listening to all those stupid podcasts and read more."

Like he was performing a magic trick, Daddy reached into his inside jacket pocket and pulled out a room key. "I forgot about this."

Within seconds, we were inside a suite with a large seating area, conference table, 80" television monitor, and two bedrooms.

I found Quentin asleep in a king-size bed with a thick, fluffy comforter pulled to his chin. He looked like a child. Before I could get nostalgic, Daddy's booming voice entered the room. "Get up, boy. You don't have time to sleep. All the trouble you've caused, you shouldn't be able to sleep again, ever." I recognized the voice from the scoldings of my youth. He could have been talking to the teenage me. *Maybe he was.*

Quentin jumped from the bed, wearing underwear. "Go put some clothes on," Daddy ordered.

We waited patiently while Quentin showered, dressed, and came out of the bathroom wearing Jack's clothes. Daddy gasped. "Damn, you look like him. How could I not have seen it?" He hesitated. "No, you look *just* like his brother. He was trouble, too."

89

Jack parked in front of the Williams family home. The house, on a street with abundant, evenly placed mature trees, was the most stately in the neighborhood. Jack remembered being a regular visitor to the Williams home as a child and a young man when he and The Judge were nearly inseparable. After The Judge married and started a family, Jack was not there as much, but the two friends remained close.

The Judge refused to sell the house after his wife died. He held on even after he moved to Florida. Jack thought he just couldn't give up the memories of the time he was Mr. Big Shot.

As a youngster, the magnificence of the home intimidated Jack—a long way from his family's overcrowded apartment, full of noise, unpleasant smells, and bugs.

A hired married couple maintained the Williams house while Jack was away. The wife opened the door and escorted him to the morning room. He found The Judge reading newspapers.

He offered Jack a seat and a cup of coffee without looking up from the newspapers. "It's a shame you have to read at least three newspapers to understand what's going on in the world today." He arranged the papers in a neat stack before lifting his head to look at his old friend.

"You know, Jack, when you were a little ghetto kid following me around, my mother would warn me I should be careful because families like yours don't carry anything but bad luck.

"Mother was convinced you would become a criminal like the rest of the vermin in your family. My father would tell her she was wrong. The criminal convictions of your brother didn't dim Dad's optimism about your future." The Judge got up from the chair and paced. "Dad was so proud when you got an Associate's Degree and joined the police force. I was jealous of how little you needed to do to impress him."

Jack noticed how much the house he remembered so fondly changed since his younger days. It seemed smaller, dingy, and confining. Where it once looked luminous, spacious, and smelled of fresh flowers, it now looked grim and smelled of dust and depression.

"Are you here to tell me what I already know, Jack? Did you come here to tell me what Ashley took such satisfaction in telling me last night? Information neither my daughter nor my best friend thought I should know. Information they kept secret for 32 years so it could be used to clobber me when I was old and vulnerable? Did you come to confess to being a child molester, Jack?"

"Yes and no. First, I wasn't a child molester. I had sex with Lyla once. I was drunk and didn't know it was her. When Lyla told me she was pregnant, she said she wanted an abortion. I gave her the money and offered to go with her to the clinic. She took the money, said she didn't want me around, and instead went to Arizona. I didn't know she had the baby.

"For several years after, I didn't see her much.. She started talking to me again when she needed help on the Bollinger case. Lyla never mentioned a baby. It was like nothing happened and I respected her actons.

"Although I often wondered why he and Lyla seemed so close, I didn't know he was my son until a few days ago. He has his birth certificate and a DNA test."

Jack waited for The Judge to respond, but his friend didn't move from being hunched over the dining table with his head in his hands. When he looked up, tears were in his eyes. "You didn't think to tell her parents what was happening with their teenage daughter?" he said bitterly.

"No, I didn't. Lyla might have been young in years, but she has been mature in her thinking since she was a little girl. I felt like she would tell you if she wanted. She arranged everything herself, even before she decided to go to Arizona. She also arranged for his adoption."

The Judge finally spoke, "Well, he seems like an intelligent young man. His criminal tendencies must have come from your side of the family.

"The 'Yes' part of this visit must have been your confession. What is the 'No' part?"

"Quentin isn't guilty of Anthony's murder. There is solid evidence to prove it."

In command of the room, Daddy grabbed a glass from the bar and poured himself a drink. We all sat in the hotel suite, waiting for his direction. My father was sober. Looking at the generous pour in his glass, I was worried if his sobriety would last. He'd been through a lot in the past few days and must have been out of his mind with grief and confusion.

"Jack told me about Quentin's parentage earlier this week. Before the media started blasting it internationally, I'm glad it got to me first. I was and am shaken by the news. 'I'm not quite ready to say, 'Welcome to the family, Quentin.' We can talk more when things settle.

Daddy continued, "Jack told me he had information to prove Quentin's innocence. He didn't share it with me. Did he talk to any of you?"

No one responded. "Well, I guess the information died with him."

"Lyla, do you still use Sam the Spade for detective work?" Daddy asked.

"Sometimes, for small things like picking up legal documents. He's pretty old, Daddy. He's still very alert, but occasionally, he gets things wrong."

"He may know someone in the evidence room. Nancy, call him and ask if he could get someone to let Jack's son look at his father's phone."

"While she's calling Sam, I'm going to get Jack's extra key. He gave it to me in case of an emergency. I guess this qualifies."

The Judge sat with his newly discovered grandson in a secluded area near the evidence room. He stared at Quentin and tried to gauge his feelings for his newly discovered grandson. It was hard not to resent him. *His foolishness has led to the death of my best friend, my last connection to my youth. The person who always stood by me through tough times.* Yet, Quentin aroused new, familiar feelings. *Will I come to love him?*

Sam the Spade provided surveillance while Quentin scrolled through the call log on Jack's phone. Jack wasn't much of a talker. Most of the calls were a minute or less, but the pattern changed during the last few days of his life. There were three long calls between Jack and a telephone number Quentin recognized as Millicent's. Several calls were to telephone numbers in the Caribbean, five different numbers. He called one number twelve times. Judging by the length of the connection, his calls weren't being answered—except for one. This call lasted nearly two hours. And there was a twenty-minute call with Nancy.

His emails were all work-related and focused on his retirement planning. He planned to move to the islands. His only texts were to his housekeeper. The last text asked her to put clean linens on the bed.

The Judge interpreted the calls. "He was trying to reach Gigi. He called her and several relatives but wasn't getting a response. When her phone was finally answered, she must have provided a boatload of information. Looks like he called Millicent shortly after. Probably to share or verify some of the information. Then he called Nancy. They talked for quite a while."

Lyla

Jack's apartment was neat. If the furniture was more tasteful, it might have served as a display apartment. Wearing my crime scene gloves, I checked the mail on his desk, mostly credit cards and utility bills. Nothing unusual on the credit card bills, but I didn't expect to see recent payments to high-end restaurants. Jack was a diner kind of guy.

His bedroom was spare. A few pictures of what looked like nieces and nephews lined his dresser. Three white and three blue dress shirts were hanging in his closet, along with two suits—one blue, one black. Jack's look was polo shirt, sweater, and blue jeans. I found those neatly folded in his drawers. I also found several condoms in his sock drawer. Jack never mentioned a lady friend. The condoms prompted me to examine the bed linens. Since Jack was hetero-sexual, he would have a lady friend. What appeared to be cum stains were on the bedsheets.

I checked the other drawers and the bathroom. There was no other evidence of a woman present. Clean sheets lay folded on top of the clothes hamper, ready to replace those on the bed. Jack wouldn't sleep on the dirty linens, so this liaison must have been recent and probably his last. I took the dirty sheets and remade the bed before I left.

Nancy had contacts at the police lab, so I asked her to have them tested.

* * * *

AFTER DROPPING THE linen at the office, I came home to find Quentin alone in my apartment, watching the news. "It's still about me." his voice was near cracking. "I guess my legal career is over. Even if I am found innocent of Tony's murder, I'll for sure be convicted of the money laundering charges."

"Not with me as your lawyer. I don't know what you planned to say to the police, and I don't want to. It's a good thing you didn't make it inside. In my view of the case, you were simply facilitating the investments of your stepfather.

"Think, Quentin. You know as well as I that people who do even a little wrong take their guilt beyond seriously. That's what you're doing now.

"For sure, you did some stupid things. For instance, sleeping with Carol. Did you know she and Tony were connected to a drug family?"

"I would be lying if I didn't say I had suspicions. But I ignored them."

"Because you were pussy whipped."

"No, Lyla. Because I was stupid. And in love for the first time."

"Thank God I never got that illness."

I stared at the sad-looking young man whose life was crumbling brick by torturous brick—seeing him for the first time as his publicly acknowledged mother. I felt different since the secret was out. A welcome release. But did I feel anything beyond?

"The Judge said it's important for me to start referring to you as some version of mother in public. Ok with you?"

"You might as well. Everyone else is. Just don't call me Mommy." I tried to sound cheerful.

He smiled and said, "The Judge is with Millicent. Jack's last call was to her. Daddy will be here at any minute to tell us what she said."

Daddy walked in as Quentin finished the sentence. First, he poured us all a drink, then he blurted, "There's a hit out on you, Quentin."

"No shit," Quentin said. "I've been shot at twice, and Jack killed while standing beside me. Somebody's for sure trying to make me dead."

"Well, whoever it needs to go back to hitman school. Missing twice? Must be an amateur," Daddy said.

"I understood the hit on Quentin. He handled some investments. But why kill Jack?" I asked.

"Millicent had no idea, either. Jack called her the evening before he was killed. He wanted police security and a safe house for Quentin.

"She arranged for Quentin to go to a safe house after the confession. She regrets she didn't move faster."

"Quentin, call Nancy. We can take you to the house where she stashed me. It's secluded, hard to find.

"Daddy, can you call Sam the Spade? We need some heavies around for security, and Sam will get people we can trust."

Sam's people arrived within an hour. No word from Nancy.

Dad was back in charge. "Have the guys take Quentin to Sam's office 'til we hear from Nancy. They won't think of looking for him there, at least for a while.

"Quentin, go down the back steps to the garage. Make sure nobody sees you. Ride in the back of the car on the floor. Sam's guys are parked in the garage. Stay away from the cameras."

* * * *

NANCY, NANCY, NANCY. Where are you, Nancy? After Quentin left, I called Nancy five times with no answer. The only time she ghosted me like this was when she shacked up with whatever "boo of the week" she was stringing along. Worry replaced the irritation I felt when she didn't answer. Driving to her house, I became frantic.

Nancy's place was on the third floor of a four-story apartment building. Pumped with natural adrenaline, I ran up the steps. I was breathless, hands shaking and heart racing when pulling her keys from my purse. I noticed the door was open.

My friend lived in an elegant three-bedroom apartment—large for a woman who lived alone, seldom entertained, and didn't have a large circle of friends and family. Antiques, art, and hand-woven area rugs adorned the place.

I called her name and got an earful of silence until a female voice from the back of the apartment yelled. "Call an ambulance!" It wasn't Nancy's voice.

I ran toward the master bedroom but found Nancy in one of the guest rooms lying spread-eagle across the bed with a woman on top of her administering CPR. I called an ambulance.

• • • •

SOMEWHERE BETWEEN JACK'S death and finding myself once again in a hospital emergency waiting room, I lost my sense of time. My world was hazy, my memory vague.

I remember being told I couldn't ride in the ambulance since I was not a relative. I don't remember how I got to the hospital. The woman trying to save Nancy must have driven me. She must have left shortly after we got there, since I have no memory of her after I arrived.

I was told Quentin was next of kin on her medical records. I heard words like overdose, Adderall, prednisone, suicide, and wait until we get more information.

I paced until my high-heeled feet throbbed, sat in plastic chairs until my butt hurt, stared into space, and tried not to cry.

Hunger was not on my mind, but one of the nurses suggested a candy bar. My reflection at the snack machine revealed Quentin standing next to me. I was so happy to no longer be alone. I hugged him. He hugged me back.

"Do you know what happened? Was someone trying to kill her, too?" I asked, afraid of the answer.

"From what they told me, this was a suicide attempt."

"But why?"

• • • •

QUENTIN GUIDED ME TO a chapel near the emergency room. It was empty. Its silence was comforting. My son held my hand. "There are things she wanted to keep to herself, Lyla. But now is the time to share. Nancy had terminal cancer."

I gasped as much from the news as learning I didn't know.

Quentin continued. "She battled it several years ago and won. It came back.

"She was too scared to go to the doctor when she noticed the signs. The cancer was very aggressive, and it was too late for surgery to help.

"She only told me. And maybe Jack. You were involved with the Bollinger case and she didn't want you to worry while you were so busy."

"Jack. . . ?"

"Yep, and for a long time. They started their relationship several years ago. She told me about it when I went to her and confessed my involvement with Carol."

Quentin hesitated and turned away from me before saying, "She told me she loved Jack. Before the cancer returned, they were planning a life together. She also told me he had been in love with Gigi for years. According to Carol, Jack and Gigi had been spending time together recently."

I didn't understand any of this. My friendship with Nancy endured almost as long as we'd been alive. We met in second grade. I loved her, and she loved me. We looked out for each other through celebrations, crises, and heartaches. How could I not know all this? How was I so blind?

A nurse tiptoed into the chapel. "Doctor will talk to you shortly. He'll meet with you here if it's ok." She was speaking to Quentin. I felt she recognized, without even knowing me, what a piss poor friend I was.

The doctor, sitting on the pew in front of us, turned to speak to me. "I wish I had better news," he said. "Ms. Lewis is in a coma. She took a great deal of Adderall, along with some other painkillers. A good deal of time passed before her neighbor smelled smoke and decided to investigate. Ms. Lewis left a pot of water on the stove. We think her suicide decision was spontaneous. She decided to take the drugs right after she put on the water and collapsed in the guest room on her way back to the kitchen to turn off the stove."

Quentin asked, "What is her condition?"

"She's in a coma," the doctor responded. "There is very little brain activity." He continued to hold his gaze on us as he said, "I have seen very few people recover from her level of drug overdose. And cancer has spread even further." He turned to look at the cross above the altar. "But, I believe in miracles. We just have to wait and see."

Nancy died six hours later.

I called Nancy's sister. We waited for the family to arrive before leaving. They all greeted Quentin by name and gave us both hugs. They were always nice to me, but I wondered at their closeness to Quentin.

• • • •

WE LEFT AS NANCY'S relatives filled the hospital waiting room. Quentin wanted to retrieve some things before the family descended from Nancy's apartment. "There are some things she wouldn't want them to have," he told me.

"You and Nancy were closer than I realized," I said on the drive to the apartment.

"She tried to fill the void left after you didn't want to be my mother. Nancy recognized my thirst for family relationships with black people.

"My parents were white people who tried to ignore race. They loved me but sometimes unconsciously said and did racist things. They once innocently thought it was cute to darken my skin, put on red lipstick, and dress me in a jockey suit with a cap for Halloween. I was about nine.

"The worst part was that I didn't know why the other trick-or-treaters laughed at me, called me 'nigger'. When I met the two of you, I was confused. I spent my life as an outsider. I was searching to belong to something—someone.

"Nancy introduced me to her family, took me to her church, and introduced me to traditional black foods, art, and history.

"Her guest room became my bedroom when my parents' home was too stifling." He smiled. "My mother thought you were trying to take me from her. Between my time with Nancy and my recent obsession with Carol, I was seldom home."

• • • •

I WAITED IN THE LIVING room while Quentin searched the drawers and closets for personal information. He came back with a folder of papers and a letter addressed to me.

Hey Girlfriend,

I know this is a surprise. As I'm sure Quentin has explained by now, the cancer has returned. I'll soon enter a stage of rapid mental and physical deterioration and pain. I cannot face it, so I decided on assisted suicide. It will be easier for us all.

Quentin has all the information on the procedure as well as all the paperwork that will need to be filed after my death.

My will, life insurance, and burial plans are in a safe deposit box; Quentin has the keys. He will inherit all my assets, including the apartment. It's already in his name. I transferred all my property to him when I got my diagnosis.

Quentin has also probably told you about Jack. All I can say is, "shit happens."

Lyla, don't blame yourself for any of this. I didn't tell you because I couldn't bear to see you take on the burden of dealing with my health. Please remember our friendship has always been the most important thing in my life. I love you.

You will probably find evidence of some illegal activities undertaken by Jack and me. You will not be implicated. Quentin has unknowingly played a role. Jack can explain.

One more thing: I have tried to stand in for you with Quentin, but I am no substitute. He is desperate for you to love him.

Nancy

· · · ·

QUENTIN CLEANED THE burnt pot while I absorbed the contents of the letter. "She boxed some letters, pictures, and souvenirs she thought you would want. She prepared everything," he said.

"I see. This letter was written before any of this stuff with Anthony's murder happened. So, I guess Jack's death pushed her to this."

"Maybe." He handed me Nancy's phone. "She hadn't listened to her voicemails. There are three from you and one from Jack. I am going to play the one from Jack."

His voice came through the phone's speaker with the same tone and confidence as if he were in the room with us. "I'm about to take Quentin to the police station. I think he'll be safer in jail for a while. Also, I need to talk to Ashley and Millicent. There is a security camera at the house in the backyard across from Lyla's old house. It has footage of the killers leaving Anthony's house. The homeowners let me see it, but they won't turn it over without a subpoena. I've spoken to Millicent. She can request the subpoena but thinks Ashley will be stubborn.

"Lyla and her father need to step back for a while. Me, too. Let the publicity wear itself off. Millicent might be willing to help tie up the loose ends."

· · · ·

MILLICENT WASN'T ABLE to get the tapes until two days later. She couldn't officially let us see them until after the DA had reviewed them and filed as evidence, but she agreed to meet us at my old house so we could get a preview. "I'll call you when I leave for the neighbor's house," she said, "but I can only give you a few minutes to look at them before the uniformed officers get antsy. If Ashley thinks I've interrupted the chain of custody, we lose everything."

Daddy, Quentin, and I were waiting in the kitchen, careful to stand away from the spot where Anthony died, when Millicent arrived through the basement door. She opened her laptop and played the surveillance tape. The image was small, so she enlarged it. We recoiled from the laptop screen.

We didn't have time to be shocked before the shooting began.

Jean-Rene burst through the front door with a gun. Gigi was behind him, shooting toward me. She missed once, then again. Jean-Rene raised a gun to shoot Quentin, but not before Millicent shot Jean-Rene in his beautiful face with her service revolver.

In the melee, Gigi had fallen to the floor. Her gun slid toward me. She tried to reach for it, but I grabbed it, aimed for her head, and shot her.

. . . .

I WAS INSANE, BAT-SHIT crazy. Or, at least, that's what I planned to tell the police when they arrived.

I sat on the steps, put the gun on my lap, crossed my legs, and waited for law enforcement. There was no doubt I shot Gigi when she was unarmed. She might have been still alive. I didn't know. I barely glanced at her when I walked from the house.

. . . .

THERE WAS NO DENYING what happened. Not only was a police detective one of the witnesses, but I had gunpowder residue all over my hands. I could smell it.

So, just how crazy should I be? I wondered as sirens approaching the house. Should I be raging, pulling at my hair, or quiet, catatonic? Suffering from PTSD? My symptoms needed to get me to the hospital rather than jail. I chose catatonic. When the paramedics ran past me to get in the house, they saw a woman not moving, looking straight ahead. I also wasn't moving when they tried to wheel Gigi (*she lived!*) past me and to the ambulance. Quentin helped me back inside the house. I made sure to be listless.

When they hadn't moved Jean Rene's body, I assumed he was dead.

· · · ·

I SAT AT THE KITCHEN table; Millicent, the star witness, sat across from me, eyes filled with sympathy. A new detective, someone I'd never met, asked Millicent what happened. *Gigi came in the door with a gun raised toward Ms. Williams. She got off two shots. Both missed. Jean-Rene came right after with a rifle. I shot him. Somehow (Millicent didn't know how I got the gun), Ms Williams had a gun in her hand and shot Gigi.*

They asked me to describe what happened. I was still out of it. Quentin whispered, "Your father is coming." I didn't move a muscle.

He raced to his parent's home, escaping before the police noticed his presence. *I don't understand. Why did my father kill Anthony? How did he even know Anthony? What the fuck is happening?*

Quentin tried to remember the few seconds before the shooting started. They were all paralyzed by shock after watching the video on Millicent's laptop. The video was fuzzy but clear enough to distinguish Fred leaving the murder scene by the basement door and walking through the back gate to the alley. He appeared to be walking toward a car, barely visible on the screen. What was probably the murder weapon was in his hand, wrapped in what looked to be paper towels. No. They weren't paper towels; they were the foot coverings Fred and Eleanor made everyone wear when entering their home.

· · · ·

THE ATMOSPHERE IN QUENTIN parent's house felt normal. Eleanor was seated at the kitchen table watching a game show. Her caretaker was beside her. Fred was pouring himself a cup of coffee.

His mother didn't seem to notice his entrance, but the caretaker gave him a big smile, "I'm so glad you're here. We've been worried."

Fred ran to him, wrapping his son in a bear hug. Quentin noticed how strong the arms were on his short body, probably from lifting Eleanor as her brain functions gradually deteriorated.

Quentin sent the caretaker home before asking, "Why did you do it, Dad?"

"To protect you," He said casually as if answering a question about the weather. "Only, I just made things worse. We knew Lyla had involved you in some dirty stuff, but we didn't realize how much her ex-husband and his new wife were involved in the drug business. At least not until after Anthony died."

"What made you think Lyla was a criminal, Dad?"

"You would bring boxes home from the office and store them in your room. Before your Mother could no longer climb steps, she opened one of the boxes and found it filled with hundred dollar bills. You know how nosy she could be."

It was coming together. Nancy would sometimes ask me to bring sensitive files home. Being a lowly associate, she thought no one would think to look in my home for information. Usually, the boxes were there for only a few months and replaced with others. I never expected the boxes to contain anything but files.

Was Nancy engaged in money laundering?

"We were worried," Fred continued, "but not panicked until you started spending a lot of nights away from home. That's when we hired a private detective to follow you. He told us you were having an affair with that Carol person. He also told us she and Lyla's ex-husband were part of a drug family.

"I decided to confront Carol to get her to leave you alone. That's why I came to the house. The ex-husband was in the kitchen, talking on the phone, when I came in. He knew who I was and laughed.

"He said, 'Come to get your boy?'

"He laughed again. 'Well, sorry. He's too far gone. You can go upstairs and pull him out of the bed with my wife, but that's not gonna stop all the other trouble he's in. He's blind with love. I know you've been having him followed, but if you try messing things up with my business, he goes to jail.'

"'He was so calm, speaking so pleasantly. Quentin, you didn't matter. Sleeping with his wife didn't matter. He thought it was all funny.

"'Go home,' he told me, 'and when he gets through screwing Carol, she'll send him right back to you.'

"He thought that was especially funny. He was so busy laughing he didn't notice I had reached into my sock and pulled out my knife.

You know, the one I brought back from Vietnam. The one I carry when I go out at night. I aimed it right at his heart. It took him a minute, twisting on the floor, but he died. I put on my shoe coverings, pulled my knife from his chest, took another knife from the drawer, and used some dirty clothes in the laundry room to wipe some of the blood from my knife onto the other knife and left."

"I knew they were criminals, so I came prepared for trouble. I didn't think I would kill somebody. He made me angry. With all that laughing. I shut him up."

I may not be much on the dance floor, but when it comes to spinning the legal system, I am Michael Jackson and Fred Astaire combined—a fleet-footed dancing machine.

Because of my obvious PTSD after the shootings, the court placed me on a seventy-two-hour psychiatric hold in the hospital. Daddy had me out in five hours by promising to have the necessary tests done by my therapist.

By the time I got released from the hospital, and Quentin was hiding.

Wounded, not killed, Gigi, not surprisingly, showed a willingness to speak to the police. She wanted police protection for Carol.

It took me two days to develop a cogent brief for presentation to the court first and the media second.

Daddy visited Gigi and got the basics of an elaborate money-laundering operation led by my accountant ex-husband. "It was very simple, elegant in fact," she said. "We would deliver the money to either Nancy or Jack. They would hold on to it until Tony could invest it in start-ups, real estate, or otherwise launder it. Nancy helped with whatever legal paperwork they needed. She sometimes enlisted Quentin's help with issues like title transfers or incorporation papers. He didn't suspect what was going on. Thought he was doing Nancy a favor by helping ease her workload.

"My father wanted Quentin involved to keep Jack and Nancy in line if things started to fall apart.

"We all thought Quentin killed Tony not because of Carol but because he caught on to what was happening. My father decided that Quentin would talk if he got arrested and ordered him killed. Once we found out about Jack bringing him to the police, my father wanted him gone, too.

"Jean-Rene was brought in to kill Quentin. After he failed, I was ordered to handle it personally. We knew Lyla and Quentin were in your old house but Millicent's being there was a surprise."

• • • •

AFTER DADDY FINISHED giving me Gigi's story, I wanted to know how Nancy got involved. He said, "Jack recruited her." He kept in touch with Gigi over the years and helped Anthony become the accountant for small businesses like restaurants, taverns, and dry cleaners in town. They also developed a network of bank and credit union employees who wouldn't ask too many questions about unusual deposits.

"Jack and Nancy were saving money for their retirement. If the feds don't attach it, Quentin has become a rich man."

• • • •

DADDY PRESENTED MY brief to the court. I was never charged for the "self-defense" shooting of Gigi. My therapist, however, recommended a three-month stay at a mental facility for intense therapy to help with my PTSD.

Because he cooperated with the police and was ignorant of his misdeeds, Quentin's money laundering charges were reduced to misdemeanors. Thanks to Daddy's influence with the bar association, Quentin kept his law license.

Carol and Gigi were deported, but not before Carol showed up at my office to declare her love for Quentin and ask for his forgiveness. I decided that information didn't need to be passed on.

Quentin spent most of the months it took to settle legal matters "out of the limelight" in Millicent's apartment. He took personal responsibility for protecting Fred and Eleanor and requested Daddy's help. Quentin's adoptive father was convicted of involuntary manslaughter and sentenced to live in a state-operated care facility with Eleanor.

Daddy is a brilliant lawyer.

After Carol and Gigi got deported, we scheduled an in-depth interview on one of the morning news shows. Quentin and I talked about the value of adoption and how giving women "choices" was good for society. Interviewing Fred from the nursing home, they heard about the joy Quentin brought to him and his wife. They would do anything to protect him. Regarding the crimes, of course, drug-related criminals are nasty people to stay away from at all costs. My poor, dead ex-husband was a victim of his family's wicked ways.

Quentin's lovely, charming face graced millions of screens. He called me "Mom" several times as I held his hand and gazed adoringly at his face. The media had one last round of what had become gossip reporting. The story would follow us for the rest of our careers, but the visibility increased my name recognition, and the scandal helped attract curious clients, many with money. As expected, my law practice flourished.

. . . .

ACCEPTING QUENTIN WAS as innocent as we portrayed him to the court was difficult for me. He was too smart. My father felt the same way, although he based his opinion on genetics. "No one in our family has ever been so blind to what was happening around him."

My opinion was based on my experience with Quentin over several years. An astute, wise, and careful lawyer. The level of ignorance exhibited in this scheme contradicted the young man I now call son.

. . . .

BECAUSE OF MY "PTSD," the court ordered me to get psychiatric counseling. Ignoring all my recent trauma (losing two of my best friends, being shot at, shooting someone, etc.), the therapist, either bemused or unusually enlightened, started our first session by saying, "Let's talk about your son. Tell me about Quentin."

116

Did you love *The Dancer - A Murder Mystery*? Then you should read *Swimming Through Mud*[1] by RoseMary Covington Morgan!

[2]

Swimming Through Mud

It's the 19th Century in America, perhaps the most pivotal, divisive, and violent period in American history.

This book introduces you and follows three young African Americans as they navigate life during the turmoil dividing the country between 1845 through 1876. A time crucial to seeking the opportunity to determine the direction of their lives and hoping to establish their rights as citizens.

We meet George, Pauline, and Gee at 17, 15, and 8 years old when, as most young people, they are full of hopes and dreams. We get to know and understand them through their fascinating journey

---

1. https://books2read.com/u/3Lx2aJ

2. https://books2read.com/u/3Lx2aJ

through adulthood. We join them as they experience the joys, loves, and tragedies of pursuing dreams through acts of prejudice, and hate.

Read more at www.rosemarythewriter.com.

About the Author

After retiring from a career devoted to developing transit projects, RoseMary Covington Morgan began her writing career in 2019. Since then, several of her short stories have been published, including The Song in the anthology Storytellers-Tales from the Rio Vista Writers' Group, School Shopping, 'Twas, and My Big Red Shadow in the Northern California Publishers and Authors (NCPA)anthology publications and two poems in NCPA publications. Also, The California Writer's Club published her short story Minnow Mildred in their 2022 literary journal, Visions.

RoseMary was born in St.Louis, MO, and has lived in Peoria, IL, Cleveland, OH, and the Washington DC area. She currently lives in Elk Grove, CA.

Read more at www.rosemarythewriter.com.